A lone jogger ran toward her. Catching a glimpse of long muscular legs, bare torso and a baseball cap turned around backward, she tried to concentrate on the task at hand. But those legs were a definite distraction.

"Hi there." He waved while he caught his breath. "I'm the camp's doctor, Mark Collins."

"Oh," she said with a nod, and then sat upright as the realization of what he'd just said hit her. *"Oh."*

He was *so* not what she'd expected. From what Vicki had told her about her new colleague and his extensive professional experience, she'd thought him to be much older than he obviously was. This put an alarming new perspective on those legs. She would be around them a whole lot more than she'd thought.

Dear Reader,

Thank you so much for reading this book. I hope that you enjoy seeing how Mark and Ellie solve the problems between them and eventually find love.

I would like to touch on a few points about the use of aromatherapy in this book. While pure essential oils and aromatherapy can certainly be used for a variety of minor ailments, and to promote positive moods, always seek proper medical attention for serious disorders first. You can add complementary aromatherapy later if you wish. There are simple ways to treat simple imbalances such as headaches and skin irritations using natural ingredients. I'm not advocating either traditional medicine or natural interventions, but instead both together to reach wellness. Lavender is my favorite of the aromatherapy oils, and helps to soothe my skin as well as my mind. Try it some time and see what you think.

There is a lot of information about aromatherapy widely available on the Internet, as well as some great reference books out there. If you're interested in using the oils make sure that you do your research first, or consult a certified aromatherapist.

Happy reading!

Love,

Molly

CHILDREN'S DOCTOR, SHY NURSE

Molly Evans

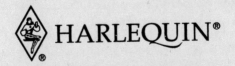

HARLEQUIN®

TORONTO • NEW YORK • LONDON
AMSTERDAM • PARIS • SYDNEY • HAMBURG
STOCKHOLM • ATHENS • TOKYO • MILAN • MADRID
PRAGUE • WARSAW • BUDAPEST • AUCKLAND

Recycling programs
for this product may
not exist in your area.

ISBN-13: 978-0-373-06746-6

CHILDREN'S DOCTOR, SHY NURSE

First North American Publication 2010.

Copyright © 2010 by Brenda Schetnan.

www.eHarlequin.com

Printed in U.S.A.

CHILDREN'S DOCTOR, SHY NURSE

CHAPTER ONE

Camp Wild Pines
Maine, USA

NURSE Ellie Mackenzie watched a man jog past the camp infirmary as she put away the medical supplies. She didn't mind the task. Frankly, it kept her hands busy and her mind off of the last difficult year of her life, which was what she needed right now. A fresh start. A break from everything that was familiar, habitual, ingrained in her by years of ICU nursing with a side dish of humility for good measure. With a quick glance at the photo of her parents that sat on her desk, she returned to her task. She liked seeing them there.

The jogger was someone she didn't know, so she didn't take much notice as he cruised by the other direction. No business of hers who was running around outside in the sweltering June sunshine in Maine. She was here to work, take a break from hospital nursing for the summer, chase healthy kids around for a few weeks and forget about the recent emotional traumas that had nearly broken her spirit. The man was probably just a counselor enjoying a solitary run before the campers descended tomorrow. After that, there would be no peace and quiet for anyone until the end of summer. At least, that's what her friend, Vicki, had said. Vicki had been a nurse here for several summers, so she should know. Now that Vicki and her husband, Sam, had had a little girl, and Sam had entered a new residency program, they couldn't spend their entire summer here. That's how Ellie had been recruited for the job.

Ten minutes later, the lone jogger ran by in the opposite direction. Catching only a glimpse of long muscular legs, bare torso and a baseball cap turned around backward, she tried to concentrate on the task at hand, but those legs were a definite distraction. She'd likely meet the fellow and the other staff later at the lodge, then she could put a name to the legs, er, face.

Before she finished her task, the squeaky screen door announced a visitor, and she entered the front room to investigate.

"Hello?" Audible wheezes caught her trained ears the second she entered the room.

The jogger had come into the infirmary. Sitting on one of the wooden chairs designated for patients by the front door, the man leaned forward with his hands on his knees, huffing and sweating. "Hi, there." He waved while he caught his breath.

"Hi, yourself. Are you all right?" Moving closer, she gave his thin frame a closer inspection.

He held up a hand, indicating he still needed a minute to catch his breath. "I'm good."

"You don't look good." Wondering if he were experiencing heat exhaustion, she sat on the chair next to him and checked his pulse. It was rapid, but not bounding. The red color of his face indicated he'd been exerting, but he looked as if he were starting to settle down.

Wiping away the sweat on his face with his shirt, he laughed. "Thanks. I'm not used to the humidity *and* heat here."

"Where are you from? Obviously not Maine," she said, more accustomed to it than he was having lived in Dallas, Texas, for several years.

"New Mexico." He wiped his arm across his forehead. "Hot, but not humid."

"Hey, that's cool. I went to nursing school there, but now I live in Dallas where it's hot *and* humid. Are you one of the counselors? I'm Ellie." Now that his color was returning to normal, she relaxed somewhat. Not that she couldn't handle it, but she really didn't want to have to deal with a medical emergency the second she arrived at camp and without the assistance of a backup. Since he was able to carry on a conversation, he wasn't in too much distress, and otherwise he looked healthy.

"Yes, and no. I'm assuming you're the nurse?"

His striking green eyes met hers for the first time. Keen intelligence shone from them. Another time or place she might have been intrigued, but now she looked away. Any interest in men and relationships was on hiatus for the summer. She was too tired to tackle either one. The last relationship had worn her out. Not that she couldn't admire the beauty of the male form; she just didn't want to get close to one just yet.

"Yes."

"I'm the camp's doctor, Mark Collins."

"Oh," she said with a nod and then sat upright as the realization of what he'd just said hit her. *"Oh."* He was *so* not what she'd expected. From what Vicki had told her about her new colleague and his extensive professional experience, she'd thought him to be much older than he obviously was. This put an alarming new perspective on those legs that she would be around a whole lot more than she expected.

He wiped his hand on his shorts, then held it out to her. "Nice to meet you."

Ellie shook the rather sweaty hand, then removed hers from his grip. "Same here. So, do you know Sam or Vicki?"

"Sam. We worked together for a few years at the university hospital in Albuquerque. And you?"

"I'm a friend of Vicki's. We went to nursing school at UNM together. She convinced me that taking a leave of absence and being a camp nurse for the summer would be good for me. Did you get the same line from Sam?" She smiled, suspecting that their mutual friends had begun a small conspiracy.

Mark grinned and put his shirt on. "Nearly identical. Seems they went to great lengths to find substitutes for themselves so they didn't have to come back."

"Right."

Long awkward silences bothered Ellie, so she usually filled them with idle chatter, attempting to keep her patients comfortable. She did the same now, falling back on the best technique she knew. Having a casual conversation with a stranger was something she'd learned to do. Naturally shy, it didn't come easily to her, but she'd learned to hide behind her nurse persona.

"So, are you ready for tomorrow?" she asked. "I hear that it's pure chaos the first day or two, especially with the younger campers who are away from home for the first time." Memories of her own camp experiences as a kid were good, though she hadn't gone to sleepaway camp as young as some of these children.

"Yep. Ready as I'm going to be." He indicated the pile of empty cardboard boxes strewn around the floor. "I see you've been tackling the supplies already. How about a break? Come down to the dock and meet some of the others with me? There's going to be a bonfire just for us tonight, then another one with the kids tomorrow night."

"Sounds great," Ellie said, but hesitated, glancing at the load of trash and boxes scattered about the infirmary. A job left undone was just work to do later, or for someone else to finish, and she hated leaving things incomplete. She simply couldn't do it in good conscience. The nagging voice of her past rolled through her, and she nearly shivered. She hated that voice and thought it had finally left her alone for good.

"Something wrong?" Mark asked, his eyes intense and watching her, unsettling her.

"Didn't a bonfire nearly destroy the camp two

summers ago?" she asked, trying to direct his attention away from her.

"That's what I heard, but it all worked out well in the end. Got a new soccer field out of it, too." He pointed to the fire extinguisher by the door. "There are more extinguishers around, but after that experience, it's doubtful there would be a repeat."

Ellie nodded, then stood. "That makes me feel a little better. Well, I'd better get back to it. There are a few more things for me to unpack yet." She hoped that wasn't too straightforward, but if she intended to get this project done before nightfall, she needed to keep moving.

"Want some help? I've finished my run and am happy to give you a hand." He glanced at his watch. "We've got two hours before the bonfire starts."

"No." Again, she hesitated. "I've got it." Stepping back, she moved away from him. He was a very intense man, and she didn't need that right now. She was supposed to be soothing her frazzled nerves, not getting them more so. The energy he had seemed to want to pull her in. She was here to relax, not get embroiled in other people's high energy, no matter how enticing it seemed.

"Can't I at least take some of the empties out to the recycle pile?" he asked and pointed to the stack by the door. "Won't take but a minute."

"Okay. But I've got the rest."

"After that, I'll unpack my stuff, take a shower and head down to the bonfire." He started toward the door and loaded his arms with the empty boxes, then paused. "You really ought to come down, eat some sticky marshmallows and hang out with the rest of us. You'll make everyone feel guilty if they know you're up here working while we're all down there having fun."

She chewed her lower lip, then reached past Mark to open the door for him. "Maybe. We'll see how much of this I get finished first." Though the idea was tempting, she doubted that she'd go. There was so much to do before tomorrow. There was always so much to do, and she never seemed to have enough time in her life to get everything done.

Mark strolled down to the edge of the lake just at sunset and the spectacular rays of orange, yellow and red bounced off of the gentle ripples of water. Breathing deep, he pulled in the fresh, humid air that was so different than he expected it to be. Not that he hadn't been in humid climates before—he had, all over the world, but something was different about this experience. It was fuller, fresher, much more alive than he'd remembered air ever being. Maybe he was being fanciful, but that's what it seemed to him tonight, and he was okay with being a little fanciful now and then. Kept things interesting. Life was too short to be serious all of the time. He'd certainly learned that lesson in spades not long ago.

As twilight deepened, he paused on the dirt path, savoring the moment. Night creatures crawled from their dens to explore their world and created such a symphony of sound that he was compelled to stop and listen for a few moments.

Sam had been right. This remote experience was

exactly what he needed after all he'd been through in the previous few years. Tension he hadn't been aware of holding onto began to slowly unwind, and his shoulders relaxed. The persistent gnaw in his gut eased a fraction. Working as a pediatric trauma physician was intense enough, then becoming a patient in his own hospital with a life-threatening illness had brought his world to an abrupt halt. Tension didn't begin to describe the hell he'd been through.

Now that he was past all that—three years past—he was still having difficulty getting back into the swing of having a normal life. He was no longer sure what normal really was. It was definitely not what it had been a short time ago. Nagging doubts, and the agonizing wait of two more years before his body was considered free of cancer, loomed over him every day and influenced him in ways he'd never imagined. Should he rent or have a mortgage? How much life insurance should he buy? Would he die before the tires on his car wore out? Could he engage in a short- or long-term relationship? These were at the top of the list. So many decisions were now based on his questionable longevity.

Chasing after a bunch of healthy kids all summer was going to be a monumental change for him, but one he anticipated being good.

The hoot of a night bird pulled him from his thoughts, and he continued down the hill to the fire blazing at the edge of the water. The smell of charred marshmallows was already heavy in the air, and he hoped that it would entice Ellie into joining the group.

"Hi, Mark. Glad you made it."

"Gil, nice to see you." He shook hands with the camp administrator.

Gil looked up the path. "Where's your nurse?"

"Ellie's finishing up a bit of housekeeping in the infirmary, then she'll be down." At least, he hoped she would be.

"Okay. There's a spot by me *and* the bag of marshmallows. You can join me there."

"Just what I wanted to hear." With a laugh, Mark followed the man through the tangle of people who had just plopped down anywhere near the fire. Casting one last glance up the path that had fallen completely dark, he hoped that Ellie would come. She seemed nice, and he needed to make friends with her while they were here for the summer. The community of people he called friends had dwindled during his illness, and he needed to rebuild his support system differently this time. His fiancé, who was supposed to be with him through sickness and health had they married, had bailed during his first treatment. She'd said it was because he wasn't likely to be able to father children, but now he knew better. The shallowness and insecurity he'd never seen had become blindingly clear.

Not wanting to cloud the evening with thoughts of the past, he put her from his mind and followed Gil to the fire.

Though he enjoyed the atmosphere of young adults and experienced counselors who returned year after year, something was missing. Maybe it was just because he was a first-timer here, maybe because he really didn't know the others yet, but something was out of place. Having grown up in a large family that didn't recognize boundaries, loneliness had never been part of his life, but now that was the feeling that came to mind.

Footsteps on the path and a quick, feminine curse alerted them to the arrival of someone else.

"Hello? Is this where the party is?"

Ellie had arrived. A smile covered Mark's face, and he stood. "Over here," he said and waved, hoping she'd recognize him against the backdrop of the fire.

"There you are," she said and made her way through the tangle of people seated on blankets and camp chairs. She reached for Mark's outstretched hand and grabbed on. Her touch was strong and firm.

"We've got a nice spot here," he said and eased down to the ground with Gil on one side and Ellie on the other, then released her hand. The small groups returned to their conversations now that Ellie was seated. Someone brought out a guitar and began playing softly in the background.

The slap of a hand against bare skin broke the silence, and Ellie jumped. "Ohh. I shouldn't have worn shorts."

"Bugs getting to you?" he asked and swatted away a mosquito buzzing near his ear. "They sound like tiny airplanes, don't they?"

"Yes. These critters are going to have a feast on me. I didn't have time to mix up my own bug spray today and just grabbed the commercial stuff left over from last year." She slapped again. "Obviously, it's not working."

"Maybe you have a sweeter disposition than the rest of us," Gil said and everyone chuckled. Small conversations picked up where they had left off when Ellie arrived.

"I'm an ICU nurse, so *sweet* doesn't really enter into my job description."

"Now, I've worked with plenty of sweet ICU nurses, so I'd have to argue with you on that," Mark said, wondering why she was down on herself.

There was a moment of silence before Ellie answered. "I might have been at one time, but over the years, it seemed to have gotten lost in the job, you know what I mean?" she asked, her voice softer than it had been moments ago, meant for only him and Gil to hear. The others were too far away to hear anyway. "Life gets to be about what you do, not who you are."

"Oh, I doubt that or Vicki wouldn't have recommended you," Gil said and poked a marshmallow onto a long wooden stick. "This is for you. Roast to your preference and enjoy."

"Thanks." She took the stick and focused on putting the fat marshmallow at the edge of the hot coals. "Vicki's a good friend, Gil."

"She said you'd fit right in here, and I believe her." He handed her a chocolate bar and graham crackers to go with the marshmallow.

"I hope she's right." Tucking her head, she focused on making the gooey treat.

Mark's mouth watered. "Gil, can you fix me up with some of that? I haven't had a s'more in years."

"You got it." He reached into the bag and produced

a marshmallow that he handed to Mark, then gave him a chocolate bar and a graham cracker.

Mark took the items, watching Ellie as he did. Her focus seemed to move inward as she watched the changing lights in the fire in front of them. The light picked up the reddish hues of her short brown hair. There was a simmering fire in Ellie that he saw, but she probably didn't even know about. Mark hoped for her sake that it wouldn't go out completely.

CHAPTER TWO

HAD she seriously even thought the word *relax* yesterday? Ha! There would be no relaxing at Camp Wild Pines. *Chaos* didn't begin to describe the absolute bedlam that descended on the camp when the four charter buses of kids arrived just after lunch. She'd simply replaced the intensity of the hospital for the madness of camp life. Ellie had never seen so many kids in one place before and certainly none with the level of excitement that sparked off of these campers. Someone must have fed them a bunch of sugar on the bus and let them go.

"Great, stuff, isn't it?" Mark asked her as the campers made their way to the infirmary for exams. He poked bellies, and tickled ribs, as each child made it through, then supplied all with a sweet treat.

"Great?" Ellie gaped at the line of campers, boys and girls, ages seven to fourteen, that trailed its way through the infirmary and out the door, filing all the way across the compound to the lodge, nearly a football field's length away. "Uh, that wasn't quite how I would have described it."

Mark laughed and placed the otoscope into the ear canal of the next camper and leaned forward for a look. "It's great to me."

Ellie gave him a sideways glance and raised her brows. The man obviously lived a crazed life if he thought this was great. "If you say so. Too much chaos and noise kinda makes me nervous. Reminds me too much of work." The thing she'd come here to get away from.

"The noise level with kids is always high. You'll get used to it."

"I doubt it." She'd never get used to it. "There's always too much to do, and never enough time to finish it." Hurrying, she pulled the folders for the next group of kids. "There's only a few minutes before they're supposed to be heading to their cabins, then to the lodge for the welcome reception." She looked at the line of campers and anxiety cramped in her belly. "We're never going to make it." What if they were late, what if she didn't do things the way Dr. Collins liked them, what if—

"Ellie?" Mark touched her on the shoulder, distracting her from her racing thoughts. She hadn't seen him rise and step closer to her.

"What?" She looked up at him. He was so close and tall that she felt smail in comparison. Until now she hadn't realized how different they were in height. He just kept going up.

The calm smile on his face didn't detract from the sharp assessing look in his green eyes. "Don't have a panic attack the first day. We'll be fine."

Sweat broke out on her back. Being so nervous about

everything wasn't how she wanted to be, but she didn't seem to know how to change. After so many years of being dedicated to helping others and more recently helping her parents through her father's illness and death, something had broken inside of her that she didn't know how to fix. She didn't know if it could be fixed. The last man she had been intimately involved with certainly hadn't thought so. "But the kids will be late, and then—"

"So? It's not like they're going anywhere for the next eight weeks. They can be a little late for the first meeting in the lodge, or we can do the remainder of the assessments tomorrow. Won't hurt anything."

Ellie simply stared at Mark. "Are you serious? Things need to be done on time, not when we feel like doing them or get around to it." How could he be a physician and say that?

"Ellie. We're not slacking. There are simply a few kids I want to take an extra look at right now. There are some campers with chronic illnesses that we need to follow closely over the summer, and if I document well now, it will save me a lot of brain strain later."

Looking away from him, she lowered her eyes. "I see. Sorry, Dr. Collins."

"No sorry about it, and please call me Mark." He squeezed her shoulder once in a gesture that was meant to soothe her frazzled nerves, then turned away. "Let's just get finished with what we can reasonably do, and then we'll go to the lodge with the kids." He called the next camper over. After a quick, assessing glance at Ellie, he carried on with the exams.

Before Mark finished with the next set of eyes, ears and tonsils, the paging system called the campers to the lodge. Without preamble, the kids scattered in a mob of gangly legs and arms and choruses of cheers. "Guess that settles it. Off to the lodge with the bunch of them." He popped off the cover of the otoscope into the trash bin that nearly overflowed beside him. With a look at Ellie, he bundled up the trash and placed a clean liner in the bin.

Stacks of files lay on every conceivable surface; some hung precariously from their perches, and a few had landed on the floor. Ellie hurried around the room picking up trash, putting away files, writing notes on other files. Her frantic pace nearly made him dizzy. He'd had enough of that sort of thing for a while. The change in his life over the past few years had made him much more aware of how he spent his time. He wasn't going to waste his, and he didn't want to see Ellie use up hers on mundane things that could wait. Especially when there was a bonfire waiting. With *s'mores*.

"I guess it's time to head to the lodge," Mark said and motioned for Ellie to join him by the door. Mark paused at the look of panic in her eyes as she surveyed the mess. There was something definitely going on with her and it wasn't files or organization. Getting out of a hospital environment was going to be good for her, too. That was obvious. He knew nothing about her personal life, but the signs of stress she displayed were enough to make him want to reach out to her, want to help her. "Are you ready?" he asked, knowing there could be an explosive answer at the end of that question, but he was ready for it. He hadn't grown up with three sisters without learning a few things about women.

"Uh, no." Ellie shook her head and moved back to the first pile of charts. "I can't go until all of this is taken care of. You go ahead, and I'll join you later." She picked up a stack of files and their contents slid onto the floor. "Probably much later."

He caught a glimpse of tears in her eyes before she hid her face behind the files in her arms. "Ellie, this stuff isn't going anywhere. Let's go meet the kids and let them get to know us a little. We're going to be here all summer, and the charts can wait."

"I just can't leave things undone, you know? I'm not built that way." A sigh flowed out of her. "If I leave things for later, I'll never catch up. You go ahead." She grabbed another stack of charts and began going through them. "It's practically a sin in the nursing world to leave something for the next person to do when you could have done it yourself." She clucked her tongue.

"You're not the only one here. I can help you. I helped create the mess—I can certainly help clean it up." That was logical, wasn't it?

"But that's not a physician's job. This is a mundane task that I should do."

"Ellie, we're not going to be in a hospital setting for eight entire weeks. I won't tell if you don't." Offering her an encouraging smile, he wanted her to respond, but she didn't.

She eyed the piles, but gave another heavy sigh. "I

don't know. It's a lot of work. I've always had the philosophy of '*do it now so you don't have to do it later.*'"

"My philosophy is '*don't* waste the now,' and I outrank you. Let's go enjoy ourselves. Before last night I hadn't been to a bonfire for years, and my stomach is growling in anticipation of more campfire food." He paused when she looked as if she were going to resist more. "Please don't make me give you a real doctor's order."

"What?"

Startled brown eyes caught his gaze, and he knew he'd surprised her. Good. "When we come back, we can do it together and get it done in half the time. It's not like it's an urgent matter, and there's no one from Medical Records breathing down our necks."

At that she gave a sideways smile, and her brown eyes lit up for the first time since they'd met. "You're right. I can deal with all this later."

"*We'll* deal with it. Promise. Let's just go enjoy ourselves." This was good. One small step forward.

"Okay. Let me grab a sweatshirt and my special bug spray. They ate me alive last night so I'm not taking any chances tonight."

"Sounds good."

She hurried to her room at the opposite end of the hall from his and returned in minutes. She carried a dark blue sweatshirt with an embroidered loon on it and a white spray bottle in the other hand.

Mark waited by the door, then walked with her to the lodge, wondering what could be special about bug spray. But if it worked, who cared?

The evening was pure delight. Kids ran wild through the camp, and he laughed more than he had in years. Tension began to simply unwind out of him with each passing moment. This was a good change for him, and one he hadn't realized he'd needed. Thank God for good friends who made excellent recommendations. Get out of the hospital for a while. That was the ticket. Oh, what a pleasure it was to be here and simply to be alive.

Tapping his foot to the guitar music, he wasn't watching as one small camper tried to sneak by, but tripped and landed nearly in Mark's lap. The little boy with bright red hair squealed, and Mark helped him to stand.

"I gotta use the bathroom," he said and his blue eyes expressed his urgency.

"Come on, it's this way," Mark said and helped the young boy find the restroom. This was something he knew he might never be able to do otherwise. Not necessarily help a kid to the bathroom, but help *his own child*—get up in the middle of the night with his own children, help them with whatever they needed. For a moment, despair hit Mark; the realization of what he might never have was reflected in the face of each and every camper present. He simply couldn't allow himself to indulge in a relationship when he might not live through the next few years. It wasn't fair to the woman or any children that could come of the relationship. Minutes later, the boy emerged from the bathroom and, for a moment, Mark forgot about his own needs that wouldn't be met so simply.

CHAPTER THREE

ELLIE stirred in her bed the next morning, awakening slowly as the sun crept over the windowsill to invade her room. She hadn't slept so well in such a long time; she'd almost forgotten what it was like. Events of the past few years had disturbed her wakeful time as well as her sleeping time. Maybe fresh air and the quiet Maine woods had helped. A lovely breeze had stirred the pines surrounding the infirmary most of the night, bringing with it the lonesome call of the loons that she loved. The soothing sounds must have lulled her into a state of bliss.

Living in a large city for so long had numbed her senses to what nature had to offer. Cement and skyscrapers and bright lights, and the never-ending roster of critically ill patients, had taken the place of activities she had once enjoyed, and she mourned that loss. Work, and the lengthy illness of her father, had just about worn her out, the breakup with her fiancé only compounding her exhaustion. Mourning had unfortunately become a way of life and one she was determined to shake off during the summer. She knew she would. She just had to figure out how to get started.

The framed photo on the table beside her bed had been taken when her father had been happy and healthy and that's how she wanted to remember him. Memories of his illness had finally begun to fade.

After a quick glance at the clock beside the photo, she bolted upright, panicked. She was late! Tearing off her sleep shirt and quickly dragging on shorts and a T-shirt, she raced out the door, then came to a halt.

Mark sat quietly with about ten kids who waited in a semi-organized line for their morning meds.

"Why didn't you wake me?" she whispered and patted her short, rumpled hair into place, supposing she looked like a porcupine with it sticking out all over.

"No worries. I've got things under control." He gave her a quick assessing glance and his eyes warmed, lingering on her longer than they had yesterday. The flush of heat that rushed through her wasn't entirely from embarrassment. Though she had said she wasn't going to be interested in men during the summer, Mark was intriguing her from the get-go.

"I'm supposed to pull the charts, and the meds, and have things ready before clinic. You didn't need to take clinic this morning. I should have done it." Her heart raced uncomfortably in her chest. This was her job, and the first day here she was already behind.

"Ellie, calm down." Mark handed a camper two pills in a paper medicine cup and a small glass of water. "Down the hatch, buddy." The camper dutifully swallowed the medicine. "Why don't you wake up and get something to eat? It's not a crisis that I take the morning clinic. You can have the one after lunch and the evening one if that will make you feel better. There are a few kids with allergy shots that are due, so you can set them up for the lunch clinic." He gave her a quick glance and adjusted the baseball cap on his head. So far she'd never seen him without it. If he was anything like her brothers, they had to have a favorite team cap on almost before they got out of bed.

"Thank you. I'll do that." Face burning, she headed to the bathroom and closed the door. She splashed cold water on her face, combed her hair and glanced in the mirror over the small ceramic sink. Already, on the first day of camp, she'd succeeded in embarrassing herself in front of the physician and a number of the kids. Determined not to let this setback get the better of her, she pulled herself together. One little problem shouldn't ruin, or set the tone for, the rest of her day. Think positive. Think positive. Wasn't that what she told her patients all the time? Maybe she ought to listen to her own words of advice. If it worked for her patients, it ought to work for her, right? She'd simply make it up to Mark somehow. She'd find a way. Opening the door to the shared bathroom, she re-entered the front, feeling a little better.

"Bear is the man you want to see at the lodge. He said he'd put a few things back for you if you're hungry."

"I can wait. Why don't I take over here?" she said, but as she looked for more campers, she saw that the line

had dwindled down to just a few. Mark had handled the
task without her help, and no one looked as if they
were distressed, so she relaxed a little more. Positive
thoughts. Positive energy. If she kept telling herself that,
she'd really believe in it one day, wouldn't she?

"Seriously, Ellie. Go ahead and get something to eat.
I'm good for a while." He winked at her. "After this I
think I might take a run around the camp, get my
exercise for the day."

"Yes, Doctor," she said and, with a frown, turned to
the door, but paused as she felt a hand on her arm.
Turning back, she glanced at him. They were going to
be working together for the entire summer, so she
should make a better attempt to be friends. Making
friends with a handsome man was always a good thing.

"Ellie, my name is Mark, not Doctor. Can you just
call me Mark? Please?" he asked and paused, then
removed his hand.

"I can do that," she said, then nodded and liked the
sound of his name rolling around in her head. "Where
I work not too many physicians like being addressed by
their first names, so it's just habit."

"A good habit to break, if you ask me. We're all on
the same team, right? And if Bear has any of those
Boston cream doughnuts left, snag me one for later,
will you?" He smiled and the effect made her hold his
gaze a second or two longer than she normally would
have. Though thin, he was a handsome man. Intense,
but handsome.

"Sure." The tension in her flashed away as his vibrant

energy seemed to move into her. Energy she seemed to need right now, but didn't know how to find.

"Maybe two if he has them."

That made her laugh and the sensation was warm in her chest. Laughter had been bountiful in her home as she'd grown up, and she realized now that it was somehow missing in her life. She'd become too serious and that was something she'd never wanted to be. "I'll see what he has. You might have to do an extra lap around the camp to work it off though." The man had a sweet tooth. She'd have to remember that. He was too thin by far, so if she could grab him a doughnut now and then, she'd do it. He'd been nothing but nice to her, so she could do something nice back. Perhaps her payback to him could come in the form of confiscated pastries now and then.

The lodge, a great lumbering building made of rough-hewn timber, was the hub of the compound, and she reached the front porch in minutes. The screen door squeaked as she opened and closed it, and she entered the cool interior to find the place empty. Last night, they had stuffed nearly three hundred people in here, and the din had been overwhelming. Now, every footstep echoed off the log walls. Just as she entered the lodge, a crashing clatter of pans and shattering of glass made her jump. Loud cursing and yelling followed, and she hurried over to the galley.

"Hello? Is everything okay?" She gasped as the biggest, brawniest bearded man she'd ever seen turned to face her, anger blazing in his deep-set brown eyes.

"No, dammit! I'm burned half to death." He held his right hand under the water in the sink and continued to grumble. A thin man covered by a white apron hovered a few feet away, his hands nearly choking the handle of a broom.

"I'm Ellie, the nurse. We haven't met yet."

"I'm Bear, the chief fried cook." He shook his head and continued to mutter under his breath.

"Why don't I look at your injury? Are you hurt anywhere else?"

"No, thanks. I'll be fine."

Now, she remembered something Vicki had said, that Bear took a while to warm up to people. "Vicki Walker said you make a great clam chowder," she said, hoping to distract him a little.

"She did, did she?" Bear cast her another glance. "We'll be missing her around here this year."

"She and Sam and their little girl will be up for a visit or two during the summer, so you'll get to see her."

Nodding at that, Bear turned to face her more fully, though he kept his hand and forearm under the running water. "Think you got anything in the infirmary to help a grease burn as big as this?" he asked.

"Sure. Getting it under the cold water is the first thing, for sure. Let me call Dr....Mark to come over and see you, too. I also have some aromatherapy oils that will take the sting right out of the burn and probably minimize scar tissue."

"I don't care about scars. Got enough of them already, so a few more won't make much difference." He sniffed. "Aroma-what? What's that?" Bear asked, a puzzled expression on his face.

"Plant extracts that have healing properties." She'd studied aromatherapy and used it on her father when he'd been ill, and she was now thinking of becoming a practitioner in addition to her nursing career. Complementary therapies were helpful to standard treatments, and she was a believer in them.

"Like folk medicine?" he asked and his fierce expression eased a little.

"Something like that." That was probably the simplest way to describe the therapy that didn't sound too out-there for most people.

"Okay. Phone's on the wall there." Bear nodded to the wall beside the mess of a desk scattered with magazines and paperwork.

"Thanks." Ellie looked at the numbers scrawled on a piece of paper beside the phone. Dialing the number, she waited for Mark to answer. She quickly explained the situation and hung up. "He'll be here in a minute. Only one camper left for the morning clinic."

A single nod was the only response from Bear. She noticed that he had reverted back to his tight-lipped expression again and suspected the burn hurt a lot more than he was letting on. "Can I ask you a few questions, Bear?"

"As long as they're not about my clam chowder recipe," he said.

"No," Ellie said and hid a grin, knowing that Vicki had worked long and hard to get that recipe out of him.

"They're medical questions. Are you on any medications or do you have any medication allergies?"

Bear answered her questions and a few minutes later Mark charged through the door of the lodge, carrying two medical supply packs. "I wasn't sure what we were going to need. I brought a few things, then we'll get you to the infirmary to do a full exam."

"I don't need no full exam. I just need my burn looked at." He held his hand and forearm out to them.

Ellie winced inwardly at the sight of the red, inflamed skin and took a pair of exam gloves from Mark. "Do you think it will blister?"

"Not sure. Might," Mark said and applied exam gloves before touching the wound that ran from Bear's thick fingers all the way to midforearm. "You said he put the injury in cold water right away, correct?"

"Yes. And to my knowledge, the sooner a heat injury is cooled, the better." Burns weren't her specialty, but that much she remembered and the advice made complete sense. Sometimes common sense was the best medicine in the world.

"Should I put ice on it?" Bear asked and winced as Mark touched a particularly tender spot that could have been the initial contact site.

"No. You don't want to apply ice to skin that's already delicate."

"Delicate? There's nothing delicate about Bear," the thin assistant cook said with a snort. "He's as tough as they come."

"You're right about that, Skinny," Mark said. "The

injured skin is the only thing delicate here, and we don't want to add anything too cold to it, because skin damaged by heat could then be damaged by cold."

"Makes sense," Bear said and gave a nod.

"If you have no objection, Mark, I'd like to try some aromatherapy oils on the injury, too." She chewed her lip, not sure how he would react to that request. Many doctors didn't understand, or agree with, the benefit of treatments that weren't created in a chemistry lab.

"Aromatherapy?" Mark asked with a quick glance at her, brows raised, silently asking for more information.

Clenching her hands together, she prepared to support her case. "Yes. I know it's considered an alternative treatment, but I like to think of it as complementary. I've used it successfully on a variety of ailments. No adverse reactions, either." Mostly she'd treated her dad and a few friends, but she truly believed in it. Heart racing, she hoped he would agree. She might even be able to document the use of oils on a burn for others to follow.

"Any objections from you, Bear?" Mark asked and turned the man's wrist slightly, looking at the wound that ran all the way around his wrist. "Otherwise, we'll just send you off to the ER in town."

"Nope. She said it's kind of like folk medicine, and I'm okay with that. Anything to take the sting out of it is okay with me, and I don't want to go to the ER. I got stuff to do."

"Aromatherapy is widely used in Europe, and I've used it before on burns, though not one as large as this." In the kitchen she was a klutz and had succeeded in burning herself in myriad ways, so she kept a bottle of lavender essential oil handy to treat herself with.

"Okay, Nurse Ellie. Do your thing."

Mark issued the order, and she was suddenly energized by his open-minded nature. Working with him might not be so bad after all.

"I'll be right back." She raced to her room, grabbed her kit of aromatherapy vials and quickly returned to the lodge. Unzipping the protective neoprene case, she pulled one bottle out and clenched it in her hand. "Keep holding your arm over the sink, will you? In case anything drips off," she said.

"I think you did a good job of cooling the injury right away, Bear," Mark said and stood to observe Ellie's treatment.

"Hurts like hell though," he said, grumbling, but allowed Ellie to minister to him. The first few drops of oil hit his skin and the fragrance permeated the kitchen. "You didn't tell me it was perfume!" Bear cried and tried to pull away from her.

Grabbing him by the apron front, she kept him in position. "It's not perfume. Now live up to your reputation and hold still, will you?"

"Oh, man. The guys will never let me live this one down. My wife, neither." He bowed his head and shook it in disgust, certain his fierce reputation had just been torn to shreds.

Beside them, Skinny snickered, but quieted after a glare from Bear.

"It's better than being in pain, and it's certainly better

than a burn that could scar badly and prevent you from cooking for all these campers." Gently, she used her fingers to rub the oil over all areas of the burn. "There are wonderful healing properties in this oil, as I said. Who cares what it smells like, right?"

Bear gave a sniff of lingering disapproval, but relented. "I guess."

"If it will make you feel better, you can tell people I held you down while Ellie poured it on you," Mark said.

Bear gave Mark's thin frame a glance and snorted. "Now, no one's gonna believe that one."

"I'm stronger than I look," Mark said and flexed his left bicep.

Bear barked out a laugh and shook his head. "I make biscuits bigger than that, Mark." Bear relaxed, and Ellie knew that had been Mark's intention.

The tension between the three of them eased. "Did Ellie get her doughnuts?"

"No. I burned myself just as she walked in. They're still in the cooler." He nodded to indicate which one.

Mark rubbed his hands together at that information. "Any others that you want to get rid of, like Boston cream? Breakfast was a long time ago."

"Yeah, help yourself. There's a couple left." Bear held still while Ellie wrapped a light gauze dressing to his injury.

"That ought to do it." She applied one strip of tape to keep the end of the gauze secure.

"I can't cook wearing this thing. I look like a mummy."

"Leave it on through the afternoon. Step back and just

supervise for a meal, then come see me before dinner. We'll take it off then and see how it's doing. You might not even blister," Ellie said, pleased that she'd been able to help him right away with her essential oils. The more she used them, the more uses she found for them.

"I'll see you in a couple of hours, then. Get your doughnuts, and I'll clean up this damned mess I made."

Skinny stepped forward with a grin. "I can help you, Bear, since you have a sore paw."

Bear turned quickly with a growl. "Now, don't be making cracks about me bein' lame…" Bear said and grabbed a towel with his left hand and snapped it at Skinny, but he missed by a long measure. "Put that broom to good use and help me clean this mess up."

The two engaged in what appeared to be a long-standing, good-natured argument. Thus dismissed, Mark and Ellie gathered their medical supplies and returned to the infirmary.

CHAPTER FOUR

THE chaos of the morning settled down and Ellie was able to prepare the allergy shots as well as get the normal lunch meds organized. Accomplishing the task ahead of time made her feel more in control of herself and more comfortable with the job she was supposed to be doing.

While the kids who had received allergy shots waited the requisite fifteen minutes in the infirmary to see if they were going to have a reaction to the injection, Ellie waited with them. A local reaction of warmth and swelling sometimes occurred, although there was always the potential for a serious reaction with each injection. She kept a number of EpiPens handy for true allergic emergencies. Something she dreaded happening to anyone, but especially a child.

Screams and shouts heralded the arrival of someone to the infirmary, and she was on instant alert. A counselor carrying a screaming child in his arms hurried toward the building. Ellie rushed to the door and opened it for them.

"What happened?" The boy screamed as if he'd had a leg cut off, but it was clearly intact.

Mark arrived directly behind them. "I heard the commotion from across the soccer field. That kid's got a good set of lungs. What's going on?" He instantly switched to physician mode, and Ellie was startled to see the visible change in front of her. The intensity and his energy were totally focused on the situation in front of him.

The counselor sat the boy in a chair and dropped into the one beside him. "Bee sting."

Ellie knelt as the boy held out a hand with a bright red welt forming on the back of it. He continued to cry and tremble despite the efforts of the counselor and Ellie to comfort him.

"I don't see a stinger, so that's good." She applied a numbing spray to the site as Mark watched over her shoulder. "This will make it feel better in a jiffy," she said and stroked his arm above the sting, trying to soothe him a little. "What's your name?" With a gentle hand, she wiped his tears away and pressed a cool cloth to his face.

"This is Adam," the counselor said when the boy didn't speak. "And I'm Eddie."

"Nice to meet you both. Is this your first year at camp, Adam?"

The boy nodded and leaned closer into the counselor, who hugged him. Tears continued to flow, but the hysteria had settled down to hiccups and sniffles. Ellie suspected that the numbing spray had begun to do its job. The fear would take a little longer to subside.

Then Adam giggled. And his eyes lit up. And then he pointed over Ellie's shoulder, and she turned. And she clapped her hand over her mouth to stifle the totally unprofessional giggle that threatened to burst out of her.

Mark looked like a rooster. He had taken a large exam glove and placed it over the top of his head. The fingers flopped over to one side, but each time he moved they jiggled like a rooster comb.

"That's more like it," he said and knelt beside them, still wearing the glove on his head. Adam reached out and batted the fingers, trying to make them stand upright. Mark examined the injury closely. "You're right. No stinger, so couldn't have been a honeybee. Looks like there might be two stings though. Must have been a hornet or a wasp. They're a lot nastier." He looked at Eddie. "Where was he when this happened?"

"Over at the edge of the new soccer field."

"Okay. As long as it wasn't in your cabin, although I think the maintenance guys checked all of the buildings for unwanted critters already." He patted Adam on the leg. "Ellie, got any more of that lavender oil handy?" he asked.

"Sure. Want to put some on the sting, too?" She brightened at the thought. Another use for her oil.

"Yes. The numbing spray smells so medicinal, and the oil is a much better fragrance for the kids."

"Got it." She returned in a minute with the oil and put a dab on Adam's hand, smearing it around the entire welt. "This will fix it up quick. I would like him to stay for a few minutes to make sure he's not going to have an allergic reaction." That would be a disaster if Mark weren't close to help.

"Good plan." He rose and removed the glove from his head and put it on Adam's head. "Looks better on you."

For the first time, Ellie was able to look at Mark's hair, which was a dense, thick brown and cropped close to his head. She supposed it was much easier to care for this way for the summer.

"I have some candies, Adam. Want one?" Mark asked and reached for the jar of sweets even before Adam's eyes widened. Opening the lid, he held it over for Adam to reach into and select his own. "You, too, Eddie."

"Thanks."

"Eddie, will you bring him back after dinner so we can check him?" Ellie asked.

"Sure." He unwrapped a candy and popped it into his mouth.

After a few more minutes, when Ellie was sure that Adam wasn't having a more severe reaction to the sting, Eddie picked up the boy and gave him a shoulder ride out the door and back to their afternoon activity. The allergy-shot kids also departed since their waiting time was over as well.

Mark wrote a note in Adam's chart regarding the injury and treatment. Watching him, Ellie knew she had to say something.

"I'm really surprised that you're so open to alternative therapy." She shrugged. "At least to the aromatherapy anyway."

"Why wouldn't I be?" He set the chart aside and focused his attention on her. "It's good practice to be open-minded in all sciences."

"I'm just surprised. So many medical people—nurses and doctors—discount other therapies as being whacked simply because it's not developed in a pharmaceutical lab." Thinking of it still irritated her, but she had to realize that not everything worked for everyone, and people were entitled to their own opinions, even if she didn't agree with them. Alan, her former fiancé, had had nothing good to say about the oils.

"I've heard that said about acupuncture, chiropractic and massage therapies over the years, but they've all proved their worth, haven't they?"

"You're right. I never thought about it that way, but the science of medicine continues to evolve, doesn't it?"

"As it should."

Sitting in the chair beside him, she warmed to her subject and decided to share a little of her personal experiences with him. "My dad was ill not long ago. Seriously ill. One of the best things I did for him was mix up some oils that my mom and I massaged onto his feet and hands." Talking aloud about her father made her miss him right then and a pang shot through her. Being weak and vulnerable in front of Mark wasn't what she wanted to do, but right now she couldn't seem to stop herself. "He said when the pain was coming on, he'd always take his medication, but using the oils in addition helped him relax enough for the meds to work."

"Sounds like a good plan to me. How is he doing now?" Mark blinked and stiffened, his face strangely devoid of emotion that had been so evident moments ago. His green eyes observed her, and she had a hard time holding his gaze. This was apparently becoming a difficult conversation for both of them, based on Mark's reaction.

"He died about six months ago." Tears pricked her eyes, but she didn't want to give in to them. One of the last things her father had asked of her was that she not grieve overly long, that she continue with her life, but she seemed to have become stuck where she was, unable to move forward out of the quagmire of emotions that wanted to tangle her up at odd moments.

"I'm sorry, Ellie. Is it something you want to talk about?"

"No. Not right now, but thanks." She looked down at the bottle of lavender oil in her hand and closed her fingers around it. "Fragrances are very powerful and stimulate memories that we often forget about until we experience the scent again. When I open this particular oil, I always think of what he said."

"He sounds like he was a smart man."

"He was." Rising, Ellie moved away from him and busied herself putting away the items used in the lunch clinic.

Bear arrived around 4:00 p.m. for his checkup. He nearly filled the small front room with his larger-than-life presence. But he didn't intimidate her as she'd expected. She guessed that putting *Teddy* in front of his name would describe Bear on the inside.

After applying gloves, she reached for the scissors and began to cut away the gauze wrapping. The fragrance of lavender filled the air around them and soothed her nerves.

"Careful with them scissors—I still have dinner to contend with," Bear said.

Although his eyes were serious, the words made her smile. There was a sense of humor in there, but it was buried deep beneath the beard and the brawn of the man. "I'll try not to cut your hand off." In seconds she had Bear's arm and hand open to the air again. "How does it feel?"

Flexing his fingers and making a fist, Bear moved his hand in all directions. He gave a grunt. "Hmm. Feels good. The lavender did take the sting out after a while."

"I knew it was going to work!" Excitement bubbled through her. "Let me find Mark so he can have a look."

Eagerly, she turned, but ran right into Mark, and his arms caught her before they both toppled over. "Whoa, Ellie. I'm right here."

"Oh, you have to see this." She grabbed him by the arm and led him to Bear's side. "See? I told you this was going to work."

The contrast in skin tones was obvious, but what had been a fierce red color of the burned skin had mellowed to a dark pink. The center that had been the initial contact site had also faded, though it was still richer in color than the rest.

Mark gave a smile to Ellie, then faced Bear. "My. You're right." He parked his hands on his hips and looked at the burn site. "It's nearly gone." Putting on the gloves that Ellie handed him, he turned Bear's arm toward the light to examine the area around the wrist. "I'm impressed, Ellie. Your lavender oil really worked."

"So am I," Bear said and lowered his arm to his side, then looked up at her, his expression open. "I'm grateful to you for fixing me up so quick."

"You're welcome." She handed him the remainder of her bottle. "Put some more on throughout the day today and tomorrow if it gives you any trouble." Eagerness and joy bubbled within her. Treating people that resulted in such good healing was the epitome of her work. "You have to make sure they are *pure* essential oils, if you ever use any again. And lavender is the only one you can put directly on the skin. The rest have to be diluted with another oil, like grape seed or the like."

"No tellin' how long I woulda sat in the ER." The bottle nearly disappeared in his brawny hand.

A thrill shot through her. "This was the biggest burn I've ever treated, but the oil seems to have done the job."

Bear stood. "Next time you get some, how about ordering me a bottle or two? Someone's always burning or cutting themselves in the kitchen. We'll use this one up in a hurry."

"Absolutely, Bear." She reached forward and gave him a quick hug.

Blustering at the affection, Bear patted her shoulder with his large hand. "I gotta get back to the kitchen. No tellin' what Skinny'll do without me there."

"Okay. Let me know if there's anything else you need, Bear."

"Sure will." He exited the infirmary and returned to the lodge.

Mark turned to Ellie with a grin. "That was good work," he said.

A flush ranged over her face and neck at the compliment. She hadn't been this excited over anything in a long time, and although the sensation was good, it was somewhat unfamiliar at the same time.

"Thanks, Mark." She tossed the fragrant gauze in the trash. The scent of lavender lingered in the air, and she took a deep breath. "Suddenly, the scent no longer has any sadness to it for me." She gave a laugh. "That's kind of a surprise to me."

"A good one, I hope." Mark leaned against the exam table, settling in for a chat.

"Yes."

A frown chased across her face and her eyes were wide and open, but there were secrets hidden in there. "But?" Would prodding her a little help her to open up?

"But what?"

"Sounds like there's a 'but' hiding in that statement somewhere." He had been the champion of hiding his feelings, so he recognized the same trait in Ellie.

"There probably is." Running her fingers along the edge of the table, she looked away from him. "I don't know. It's just that I've not felt like this for so long that I don't quite know how to go about making things different." She blew out a long sigh.

"Change is never easy, it takes time. I know that myself." The life he had known had been changed for him, and he'd had no choice except to go along with it. A memory shuddered through him.

"You don't look as if you've had a serious problem in your life. You're so easygoing. And Vicki told me that you've traveled in many parts of the world, gone on missions for health care and even run in two marathons."

"Well, yes, I have done those things, but the past few years haven't been great." Yes, that was an understatement. He was lucky he'd survived the past few years.

"I'm sorry. I'm prying in your personal life, and I have no business doing that." She picked up the few remaining files from the table and put them in the filing cabinet. After that, she looked around for something else, but they had finished all of the assessments earlier. He'd made her uncomfortable, and he wanted to remedy that now.

"Ellie, no." He removed his cap and ran his fingers through his hair, then replaced the cap. "I mean, yes, there are things in my private life that are painful, but no, you're not prying." He pulled a chair over and sat backward on it, resting his arms on the back. "We're going to work together for the summer, and we'll get to know each other. For now, I'll just tell you that I was seriously ill a few years ago. It came out of the blue and hit me hard." So hard he'd nearly died from it.

"I'm sorry, Mark." Tentatively, she reached out and touched his arm, offering him a gesture of comfort that he knew she would have offered to anyone. That's just the way she was, giving so much to others. "That's why you're on the thin side, isn't it?"

"Yes. But every day I'm getting healthier and stronger."

With a grin he patted his flat abdomen. "If I keep up those Boston cream doughnuts, I won't have to worry about the thin part for much longer."

"I suppose you're right," she said and gave a quick laugh. "If you're not bothered by the illness, then I won't be, either. Serious illness can take over a person's life, so I'm glad you're over yours." She gave a sigh and pulled a chair close to his. "Since you've shared some of your story with me, I'll share some of mine with you. Stress has really been getting to me the past year. My father died of cancer, and working in an ICU setting is no piece of cake. So I'm hoping that some downtime, running after healthy kids for the summer, will lighten me up a bit."

"I'm sure it will. Sounds like we're both where we need to be for a while." He puffed out a quick sigh. It was actually a relief to talk a little about his past, his illness. Not that he wanted to linger on it, but sharing a tiny bit with Ellie was not as difficult as he thought it would be.

"Definitely."

"I think I'll take that extra lap now, if there's nothing else going on."

"Nope. Just dinner at the lodge, then clinic right after." She gave a quick laugh. "No bonfire tonight though, so you'll have to indulge your sweet tooth some other way."

"I'll do that." Turning his hat around the proper way, he left the infirmary and the sudden appeal of Ellie's smile.

Since his illness and recovery he'd been too focused on survival to be attracted to anyone. Now that he was ensconced in a small building with Ellie, trapped for the summer with a beautiful woman in a remote area, he was uncertain that that had been a wise move on his part. Being attracted to her simply because she was available and in front of him didn't seem likely. If another woman had gotten the job, he probably wouldn't have found her as interesting, as intriguing, as Ellie was. She was a woman with depth and caring and didn't hesitate to share herself with others. There was promise in that. He may not be around long enough to cash in on that promise, so he advised himself to steer clear of Ellie and her allure.

After a few leg stretches, he took off at a slow pace around the camp. This time of the afternoon, the temperature was hot and the humidity was high, leaving the skin and hair sticky even after a short exposure. Dark threatening clouds gathered in groups on the horizon, and he supposed they'd have a storm before the night was through. He loved storms and the chaos they created in the skies. External chaos was good. Internal chaos was not so good.

Right now, he needed to put some distance between himself and Ellie, the source of his current chaos in feelings. The vulnerability she gave off appealed to some manly aspect of his personality. He supposed that was why he'd become a physician, because he wanted to help people. He was a doer and a fixer. And he wanted to help Ellie without getting too involved emotionally. That was the downfall of being involved with people. Unfortunately, he wasn't much of a technology man, or he'd consider research in a lab somewhere, limiting his contact with others. But he knew that wasn't going to solve his problems, and he made his way around the soccer field down the path to the lake at an easy pace.

A swim class was in full swing, and he watched the boys and girls splashing around the roped-off lanes of water. With a laugh, he recalled his swim lessons as a kid. He'd sunk like a rock and had almost given up until his gangly body had somehow managed to put everything together, and he'd made it across the pool, sputtering the entire way. From then on, he'd lived in the neighborhood pool every summer. Now, watching the kids learn their lessons, he was once again reminded of something he might never do—take his own child swimming.

As he had moved through college and residency, he'd never thought of being ill himself. He'd always thought of how he could help others, how he could use his skills as a physician. Other people got sick and died, other people contracted chronic illnesses. He'd become one of those *other people*.

Finding a spot on the dock away from the kids, but where he could observe them, he thought back to that time in his life that had nearly killed him.

CHAPTER FIVE

HE'D found a lump in one testicle where there ought not to have been one. Though he'd been in a hot shower at the time, he'd broken out in a cold sweat. He'd experienced all the phases of grief, but had set them aside in order to get a swift diagnosis and treatment. Denial was what got people into serious trouble. Denying a serious illness only gave the illness more time to grow and take over, rather than defeating it quickly in its tracks. He'd had to make a leap over that denial hurdle. Though he knew that his sort of cancer responded very well to treatment, the fear of it never left him.

The cancer diagnosis had laid his family low. His father had been absent most of his life and was no source of comfort or help then. Thankfully, his sisters had come together to help him when he'd needed them the most. Rather than tearing his family apart as many serious illnesses do, his condition had strengthened the bonds between them. Mark wondered if the same thing had happened to Ellie and her family when her father had become ill, if she and her mother were still close. Of course, he'd seen the picture of her parents in the workroom, but she hadn't mentioned her mother at all.

The swim coach blew her whistle, redirecting Mark's thoughts as she called the swimmers from the water. The kids landed in sloppy, wet piles as they sat on the dock and listened to the instructions.

Rising from the wooden dock, Mark knew that everyone would be called to the lodge shortly, then there would be clinic right after. He'd left Ellie rather abruptly, the story of her father's death affecting him in a way he hadn't expected. He wanted to find Ellie and apologize for being rude.

He returned to the infirmary and found it empty.

"Rats," he said.

"Where?" Ellie's voice came from down the hall.

"Where are you?" Good. She was still here.

"In the ward room."

Mark moved around the corner and found Ellie reclining on one of the beds and his stomach clenched at the sight of her there. "What are you doing?"

She held up a book and removed her glasses. "Catching up on my reading. I brought a stack of books a mile high." Closing the book, she avoided looking at him.

"Ellie, I'm—"

"Help! Where is everyone?"

Ellie and Mark bounded out of the ward room and into the front. "What's going on?" Ellie asked.

A counselor and a young male camper were in the front room. The boy was covered in scrapes and scratches. Blood dripped from multiple lacerations on his face, neck, arms and hands.

"What in the world happened to you?" Mark asked, grabbing two pairs of gloves and handing Ellie one.

"A tree happened," the counselor said with a quick glare at the boy.

"What's your name?" Mark asked and motioned for the boy to be seated on the exam table.

"Kevin." Holding onto his left wrist, he climbed onto the table with some assistance from his counselor.

"I'm Scott," the counselor said.

"So how did a tree happen to you, Kevin?" Mark asked and applied a stethoscope to the boy's lungs, looking for more serious injuries than what was already obvious.

"I was climbing and fell out."

"Right into a patch of blackberry bushes," the counselor said and shook his head.

"Ouch. That must have hurt. Why don't I start cleaning up the scrapes?" Ellie suggested. Her heart rate had jumped at first, but it settled down now that the injuries seemed benign. "So what's with the arm? Is it hurting?" she asked. Behind the red cheeks, he had a bit of pallor that made her wonder whether his arm was broken. The way he cradled it was also a classic sign of injury.

"It hurts. Hit it on a branch on the way down and the ground, too."

"Double ouch," Mark said and reached out to touch the injury gently. "Can you make a fist?" he asked and went through the examination with a tender touch.

Kevin winced and tried to pull away. "Ow."

"There's swelling already in his fingers," Ellie said and began cleaning up the scratches with gauze soaked in normal saline.

"I see that." Mark sighed. "You're probably going to need to go to town for some X-rays, Kevin."

"Oh, man," he said, his voice whining. "My mom is going to kill me."

Ellie laughed at that. "I doubt it. But we will have to call her and let her know what's going on."

"Do you have to? I just got the cast off of my other arm three weeks ago."

"What happened to that arm?" Mark asked with a grin.

A red flush covered Kevin's face and neck, and he dropped his gaze. "I fell out of a tree in the backyard."

"You're going to have to start climbing shorter trees," Ellie said.

Mark laughed and Ellie felt the first stirrings of attraction at the sound. The man had a wonderful laugh. Even though he was engaging with people, she sensed a deep sadness within him. Maybe she was wrong, or maybe it was some nursing instinct firing to life, but that was what she felt.

"Ellie, can you handle things here while I take him in for X-rays?" Mark asked. "I don't think we need an ambulance for this."

"Sure," she said. "Not much else going on right now. Just the clinic after dinner. I'll call his mom and let her know what's going on. Otherwise, if anything serious comes up I can call you on your cell phone."

"Sounds good." He let his eyes linger on her face and

mouth a moment before Ellie had to look away. Wow, the man was intense, and something in her was responding to his intensity, his energy, the vibrancy of the man. This was something she hadn't expected of her summer as a camp nurse.

"Come on, kiddo. We're going to town," Mark said. "Scott, want to come along, too?"

"I wish. I hear they have a great pizza joint in town, but I have to round up the rest of the group before they're all in the trees, too."

"Go ahead. We'll take it from here," Mark said, and Scott headed back to his group. "Pizza?" He looked down at Kevin. "You like pizza?"

"Is that a trick question? We have them in school sometimes."

"No. It's not a trick question. I should know every kid likes pizza, don't they? After X-rays we'll stop for some." Mark took a cloth sling from the supplies and fitted it to Kevin's arm, keeping the wrist higher than the elbow.

"Here's a couple of ice packs, too," Ellie and handed Mark a plastic bag filled with ice cubes. She placed another one inside the sling on top of Kevin's wrist.

"Great." They moved toward the door. "Anything you need from town?" he asked.

"Nope. We're good on everything still."

"Okay, see you in a few hours, depending on how many people are ahead of us in the ER."

With a nod, Mark and Kevin left the infirmary, and it suddenly felt too quiet and too empty. Ellie took off her gloves and cleaned up the supplies she had used, then made a quick call to Gil, then a lengthier one to Kevin's mom. Returning to her book on the ward bed, she tried to focus again on the story unfolding between the pages, but she couldn't concentrate on the characters and found herself rereading the same passage several times. Her eyes drifted down, then sprang open again as she fought off the urge to sleep.

Maybe it was too hot in here, she thought and got up to turn on the air conditioner. Maybe she needed some iced tea. A little cool air and cold caffeine should wake her up. After going to the small kitchen and fixing herself some refreshment, she returned to the ward room, but her book no longer held the appeal she'd anticipated.

What she needed was distraction from her thoughts, from thinking about Mark and that last, long, hungry look he'd given her. An involuntary shiver made her tremble, and she pressed the glass of cool tea to her cheek. No man had looked at her like that in a long, long time. Certainly, Alan never had. Maybe it was just her vanity perking up after months adrift at sea.

Something about him appealed to her. But she'd promised herself a rest for the summer, to regroup, to find where she wanted to go beginning in September. Most people thought of spring as a time of renewal, just coming out of long winters, but to her, fall was her time of refreshment and growth. The weather and season changed, kids started back to school and life seemed to have a greater sense of movement for her than in the spring. She always felt stronger and more energized with cool mornings and warm afternoons.

She'd always wanted to see the famous New England autumnal change that she'd read and seen pictures of. It seemed as if the past few years she'd lived her life by reading about places instead of experiencing them. Perhaps she could stay in Maine or the New England area to experience it firsthand this year. When the fall moved on, then maybe she could as well. Her father had left her a small nest egg that she'd yet to tap into. Until now, there was nothing that she'd really been interested in doing, just going to work. Staying over a week or two in the fall to enjoy the scenery seemed like a good use of her time and would hardly dent the money he'd left.

Returning the novel to her room, she pulled out an aromatherapy encyclopedia instead to read up on some of the new oils she wanted to try soon. Closing the book, she turned it over and looked at the front. Aromatherapy. Hmm. She loved this therapy. Maybe she could realize her dream of becoming a certified aromatherapist. The money her dad had left her would certainly fund such an endeavor. She'd look into that soon, too.

Hours passed with no word from Mark. Restless after the small clinic had wrapped up and no further emergencies had occurred, she tried to walk off her mood outside, but the mosquitoes got to her first, and she made a hasty retreat.

As darkness descended, she lunged onto the screened-in infirmary porch and shook her clothing to rid herself of any unwanted creatures. She was really going to have to remember that bug spray every time she left the building. Then she realized something was different in the infirmary. Something in the air. She sniffed.

Her footsteps hurried as she moved into the front room and her mouth began to salivate at the fragrance filling the air.

Pizza?

"Mark?" she called and looked around. Where was the man? More importantly, where was the food?

"In the kitchen."

Tossing her sweatshirt onto the back of a chair, she followed her nose to the small kitchen and gasped in surprise. "What's all this?" she asked, a bubble of warmth surging in her chest.

"It's called pizza," Mark said and turned with a glass of wine in each hand. "I hope you like red."

"I like anything called wine," she said and reached for the glass. "Oh, this smells fabulous."

"Sit down, and I'll tell you about Kevin. No sense in letting good pizza get cold."

Ellie sat in one chair and Mark in the other, around a small bistro-style table. Beneath the table, their knees rubbed, and they adjusted their positions. Reaching for a slice, Ellie bit into it. Moaning out loud, she chewed.

"I love a woman that isn't afraid to express herself about food." Mark watched her, grinning.

"I'm so sorry," she said and covered her mouth with her hand as she chewed. "I couldn't help it!" She sipped the wine that went perfectly with the pizza. "This is the most incredible pizza I've ever had, or I must be incredibly hungry. And I even had dinner."

"No. It's that good." Mark helped himself to a piece.

"So tell me what happened." Emily watched Mark as he spoke, his face animated, his story engaging.

"It's a break, but not bad. He's casted again." He shook his head. "Kevin reminds me of myself when I was a kid."

"How so?"

"Always getting into trouble in some way or another."

"You?" Ellie looked at him and tried to imagine the young version of him, but failed to see it. "Hard to imagine."

"Not if you talked to my mother. She said she kept her hair color just fine with the three girls, but when I came along, that's when things started to go gray."

Ellie laughed at that. "Was she serious?"

"She says so, but I'm not sure."

They talked a little more about Kevin's case and the plan for keeping him comfortable should the need arise for pain medication. "Should we bring him to the ward room for the night, or do you think he'll be okay in the cabin?"

"I told him that he could make that decision. He has ice packs, and I have a prescription for pain medicine should he need it. Elevation and ice are the best, but if he's anything like me, the cast won't keep him out of trouble, only delay it for a day or two."

"The voice of experience," she said and paused. Maybe it was the wine and the company, but at this moment, with nothing going on around them, she relaxed.

"More?" Mark asked and raised the bottle over her glass.

"Just a little. Red keeps me up at night if I drink too much."

"Then no more after this. Insomnia is no fun."

"Again, the voice of experience?"

"After residency hours, your system doesn't know if it's coming or going sometimes. Took a few years to get it straightened out, then being on call is no picnic, either."

"Is that why you came to camp for the summer? To get away from all that hospital grind?" she asked and watched as his green eyes clouded over. "I'm sorry. I've overstepped my boundaries with that question. I didn't mean to."

Mark reached across the small table and took her hand. "No. It's okay." He took a deep breath and sighed, wondering how much to tell her and decided there was no harm in giving her some information. "Being ill and the recovery took a lot out of me. I was hoping to recharge my batteries here over the summer."

"Have another slice of pizza," she said and slid the last one over to him.

"No can do. I'll explode if I have any more." He patted his stomach.

"Then I'll wrap it up for tomorrow. Maybe you can have it for your midmorning snack or something. That is if you like cold pizza." She reached for the last slice to wrap it up, but stopped when Mark's hand encircled her wrist.

CHAPTER SIX

"YOU'RE very sweet, do you know that?" he asked and wondered if she knew that was really true. Many women, especially caregivers, undervalued themselves and didn't even know it. They spent their energies on everyone else except themselves. His mother, his sisters—they were all like that. Not that it was his cause in life, but when he had an opportunity, he wanted to let the people in his life know they were valued.

A shadow crossed her face and puzzled brown eyes met his. This was one of the few times that she met his gaze full on and the effect on him was inspiring and arousing. Two feelings he'd not allowed himself to indulge in for a long time. But now, sitting across from Ellie on a hot summer night, having had a nice evening with her, part of him wanted to reconsider his vow not to be involved with anyone until his five years of being cancer free ended. Provided he was still living.

"What?" she whispered, her gaze locked on to his.

He didn't want to let go of the moment, but he knew he ought to. Taking a deep breath, he released her wrist and tried to return to the comfortable relationship he and Ellie had established. "Oh, nothing. Just wanted to let you know."

He stood and gathered the pizza box, folded it and put it in the trash bin.

"You know, earlier, you left pretty quickly. I hope I didn't say anything to disturb you," she said.

This time she stopped him and her touch on his skin was lightning. Unable to resist the magic in her touch, he paused and looked down at the sincerity in her expression. She cared about people. It was innate in her, something she probably didn't realize she had, and that was very hard to resist.

His vow forgotten for the moment, he didn't try.

Facing her in the small room, he paused. Her natural allure reached out to him almost as tangibly as her hand on his arm. Without taking another second to think about whether it was right or wrong, whether he should or shouldn't, his gaze dropped to her mouth, and he leaned in and kissed her.

Ellie parted her lips beneath his. Instinct made him pull her a little closer to him. The soft feel of a curvy woman leaning into his chest nearly robbed him of all good sense.

Desire vibrated through every cell in his body, but he had to step back. Ellie had been through enough pain recently. He didn't want to add to that. With reluctance, he eased back from her. "I'm sorry, Ellie. I shouldn't have done that."

"Yes, well." She stepped back from him and gave him

a nervous glance. "We're both professionals. We won't let this affect our relationship, right?" Turning away, she pulled the box of foil from a drawer and wrapped the last slice of pizza.

"Really, it's my fault, my responsibility, and I apologize for acting inappropriately." Dammit. He should have controlled himself better than that. No matter how attractive Ellie was or how perfect the moment seemed between them, he needed more control that he obviously had.

"You sound like you regret touching me." Hurt flared in her eyes before she turned away from him.

"Quite the contrary." He stepped out of the tiny kitchen that suddenly became stifling. The space was too tight and he was too close to her for his comfort. "I'll say good-night, now."

"Good night, Mark," she whispered and watched as he made his way down the hall. Just what had he meant by that comment—"Quite the contrary"? Had that meant he'd enjoyed the way the electricity had flowed between them for a moment or two? It obviously hadn't been just her that had felt that little sizzle in the air before their lips met. She'd hadn't felt that level of attraction for a man in a long, long time. And now, she wasn't sure she wanted to feel it for the man who was her coworker on a temporary basis.

Perhaps he was right. Though there was definite attraction between them, acting on that attraction might not be the wisest move that either of them could make. She placed the pizza in the nearly empty refrigerator, corked the remainder of the wine and set it in a high cupboard, then washed the glasses.

After her few tasks, she surveyed the front room. Sighing, she looked around for something else to clean up, but there was nothing. Already prepared for the morning clinic, she had nothing else to keep her occupied.

A few days passed as Ellie and Mark returned to their routine, but without the same level of comfort that there had been between them. Ellie tried to forget the feel of Mark's lips against hers, but at odd moments she'd remember and look up at him. Despite the illness he'd suffered, he was strong and masculine, and made her feel very feminine. No man had interested her much in the past year or more, and now, with Mark under the same roof as her every day, she wondered if it weren't a simple case of coveting thy neighbor, because he was close and handy to her. And she was definitely coveting.

After the lunch clinic ended and the kids found their afternoon activities, she and Mark occupied themselves in the infirmary. She sat at the table and worked on her e-mails. Mark produced some professional journals that he intended to read.

A sudden flurry of activity behind her made her turn. Mark ripped the trash bag from the metal trash can, took one of the clear liners, blew air into it and pulled it over his head.

"What are you doing?" she asked and gaped at him. "Are you out of your mind? Take that off!" Had he gone mad? Lunging toward him, she tried to rip the bag from his head. Goofing around with a glove to entertain the kids was one thing. He was going to suffocate himself with this trick.

"Call 911. Now!" His voice was oddly muffled inside the bubble of the bag, but she understood. His energy was on high alert, and she stopped struggling with him. This just wasn't right.

"Are you ill? Why am I calling 911?" Confused, Ellie backed up a step, but she still had no idea what was going on.

He tied the ends of the bag beneath his chin. "Because I'm about to get attacked by mad hornets."

"What are you talking about?"

Mark pulled the fire extinguisher from the wall beside the door. "Just do it." Moving toward her, he pressed a quick kiss to her mouth through the bag. "Bring the emergency kit and every anaphylaxis kit you've got."

With that, he raced out the door, looking like a cartoon character dashing across the yard. Horrified, Ellie watched him go, and as her focus changed and narrowed to what he had seen, she exclaimed, "Mark!" and grabbed the phone, terror filling her, and dialed the emergency number. "Oh, God."

During the quick call, Ellie couldn't keep her gaze from the scene unfolding across the compound. Mark raced toward what she hadn't seen at first. The air was dark with it.

A huge swarm of insects. Someone was fighting for their life in the middle of it.

Mark charged right into the fray, at the risk to his own

life, spraying the stinging insects with the extinguisher, trying to create some relief from the attack. Shouts and screams filled the air as others noticed the situation, and Ellie's nervous system knotted up. Counselors and campers filled the area, but the adults ushered the children away from the scene, thankfully preventing injury to anyone else.

The emergency pack was in her hand before she was aware of it and, heart wild in her chest, she raced out the door behind Mark, totally uncertain as to what to do, how to respond to this emergency. People died every year from a single sting. How someone could survive such an attack, she didn't know.

Prayers and whispers of safety ran through her mind. This was her worst nightmare come to life. Nothing in her experience had ever prepared her for this. Nearly breathless, she stopped just yards away from them as the white puffs from the fire extinguisher filled the air.

Ellie dropped the equipment and screamed, "Mark!"

As he fell to his knees, he continued to spray the fire extinguisher until it fizzled out empty. By then, the hornets, or whatever they were, seemed to have dispersed to a few confused individuals that posed no further threat.

Mark ripped a hole in the bag and tore it off of his head. He hauled in great gasping breaths, then barked out a few wheezing coughs. She hurried over to him and placed a hand on his back. "Are you okay?"

"Check…him…first," Mark said, panting to catch his breath.

She heard the wheezes as he struggled for breath. But with the injuries to the other person unknown, she had to do as he instructed. Mark was at least breathing. The bees appeared to have dissipated with the majority killed or dying from the effects of the extinguisher.

Skinny, however, lay in a heap on the ground, dead hornets all over his back.

"Skinny?" She called his name and flicked away the dead insects so that she could turn him over. "Skinny, can you hear me?" She struggled to turn the thin man over and found Mark's trembling hands, covered with welts and stings, there to assist her.

"What in the Sam Hill is going on here?" Bear yelled as he charged toward them. "Oh, my Lord!"

"There's been a hornet attack, Bear. Skinny and Mark are hurt." She took a deep breath and choked down the tears that wanted to threaten. She had to help them, and she couldn't be afraid. If Mark collapsed, too, she'd be the only one left to care for both of them. "Let's move him away from here. I'll take his legs—"

"I'll get his shoulders," Bear said and tucked his hands under the injured man's arms. Skinny was unresponsive and his head fell to the side. In seconds they had moved him away from the attack area and placed him on the ground again.

"We need help right now." Despite trembling hands, she tore open the packages of two Epi-kits, and put them together. "Talk to him, Bear. He'll know your voice. Just talk to him."

Bear muttered in a gentle voice, one she'd never

heard before, as his brawny hands brushed the hornet carcasses off of Skinny's chest and neck. Eyes, nose and mouth already swollen to an extreme, the man was unrecognizable. He was in *very* serious condition. Ellie pulled back the syringe and plunged it into his thigh, administering the lifesaving medication.

"Give him another one," Mark whispered, his voice strained. "He's gonna need it. Get the oxygen on him, then give me an injection." Though raspy from exertion, Mark's voice was almost normal again.

Without a word, Ellie administered a second syringe into Skinny's other leg. "Bear, can you rub those spots while I get the oxygen?" Nodding, Bear complied. In seconds she had a mask connected to the transport oxygen tank and cranked it up high. She placed the mask on Skinny's face, and Bear held it tight.

Turning to Mark, she winced, but tried to control her reaction.

"That bad, am I?" he asked, but the attempt at humor fell flat.

"Let me give you this, then you have to check Skinny. He's not looking good." She quickly gave Mark the shot in his left thigh and turned back to Skinny.

"Is he breathing?" Mark asked and rubbed the injection site on his thigh.

"Yes, he's got a major stridor though." The swelling of the airway caused the high-pitched crowing sound that was unmistakable in a respiratory emergency. Ellie shook her head, willing the epinephrine to start working, to start counteracting the body's natural reaction to the stings.

"Jake!" Bear called to one of the assistant cooks that stood nearby. "Go show the paramedics over here." With a nod, he ran to the entrance.

Mark crawled on his hands and knees over to Skinny's head and took over holding the oxygen mask from Bear's hands. Mark attached the ambu bag and tried to force extra oxygen through to Skinny's lungs. "His airway's constricting already. He's really tight." Mark shook his head and clenched his jaw together. "I don't know if this is going to work."

"If he loses his airway completely, we're going to have a problem." Ellie hated to say it, but the man could certainly die right in front of them, no matter what they did. "Can you do an emergency trach if needed?" Sometimes cutting a hole in someone's throat was the only way to save a life.

"Yes, but I'd rather not have to." Mark removed the oxygen mask for a second and opened Skinny's mouth to place an oral airway. It would assist in keeping his throat open despite the swelling. "Dammit. I thought this might have happened." He extracted several dead hornets from Skinny's mouth, then placed the plastic airway and applied the oxygen mask again.

"There was one in his mouth?" Ellie asked with revulsion and shivered.

"Several. I'm certain he has multiple stings inside his mouth and on his tongue. That's why his breathing was affected so quickly."

"Oh, dear."

"Can you use your purple stuff on him?" Bear asked,

his eyes filled with worry and concern for his friend, aware of the gravity of this situation. He held out his hand. "Fixed me up right quick on my burn. Can you use it on him?"

"My what?" she asked without looking up from her task, trying to get an IV into Skinny's hand. They needed IV access, and they needed it now. In the next second she had one in and taped it down.

"The folk medicine. The purple stuff you used on my burn."

"Purple stuff?" Then the light bulb in her brain went on. "Oh, the lavender oil!" Ellie glanced up at Mark, and he nodded.

"I'll bag him. Go get your purple stuff."

CHAPTER SEVEN

ELLIE raced the few yards to the infirmary and returned in minutes with her kit of essential oils. Fumbling with the zipper as the paramedics arrived, she sat the kit on the ground and pulled out the lavender oil.

Mark spoke to the rescue crew as Ellie dabbed the oil onto the stings on Skinny's face and throat, not knowing if it would truly help the emergent situation, but it certainly couldn't hurt. The rest of the stings could wait. His condition was too serious to mess around with. If he survived this attack, she could treat the welts later.

"Damned hornets. They keep on stinging. They just don't die like a honeybee," Bear said, anger sparking from his eyes. "He should never have been out here."

"What was he doing?" Mark asked and continued to bag Skinny.

"He was looking for fiddlehead ferns that grow here every summer. Since the fire two years ago, we weren't sure whether they'd come back like usual, and I just mentioned that I had a taste for some. Musta kicked into a ground hornets' nest." Bear shook his head. "They're nasty."

"Let's get him loaded." Bert, the paramedic, said and took over bagging Skinny. They headed off to the local hospital with him.

"Bear, why don't you follow along?" Ellie suggested and gathered the equipment, her heart still not back to normal, the trembling in her hands not finished yet.

"I got dinner to get going," he said, but his gaze followed the ambulance out of the camp.

"Give your instructions to one of your other cooks. I'm sure they'll want to know someone's with Skinny and everyone will feel better if you're there with him."

Bear gave her a look with his dark eyes and nodded. "You're right. They'll do better with something to keep their hands occupied." He placed his on Ellie's shoulder and gave her a squeeze. "Thanks." With that, he picked up Skinny's hat and moved off to the lodge.

Ellie turned to Mark. "Let me see to you now, please?"

"I'm going to be okay. I can feel the jitters from the epinephrine." Stooping, he picked up the fire extinguisher. "Gonna need another one of these for the infirmary."

"Later. Why don't you go shower, and I'll get the rest of this stuff?"

"Here, we can help," Gil said and stepped forward. "We'll get this stuff picked up. Ellie, take him to the infirmary. Then I'm going to call an exterminator to make sure these things are gone for good."

Stiff and sore, Mark walked toward the infirmary

building. Ellie approached his side and offered an arm of support around his waist. "Are you sure you're okay? I think you ought to go to the hospital and get checked out, too. I'm concerned about the amount of stings you've gotten, even though they aren't on your face or neck."

"You can take care of me." Unable to find the strength or desire to resist, he put his arm around her shoulders and gave her a little of his weight. Leaning on someone was not something he'd wanted to do and hadn't done in a long time. Not since his illness. But now, leaning on Ellie, having her lithe body giving him some of her strength, was just what he needed. Tremors rattled through him, and it wasn't just the effects of the epinephrine. He was exhausted from the outrageous amount of energy he'd exerted.

Reaching ahead of them, Ellie pulled the squeaky screen door open, and they entered. Guiding them straight to the bathroom, Ellie eased him onto the edge of the tub. With one hand balancing him, she turned on the taps with her other hand. "A cool bath with baking soda will help the stinging some, too. Can you manage while I get the baking soda?"

"I think so," he said. But he really wasn't sure he could get into the tub without disgracing himself or landing on his head. He hadn't needed help to undress or bathe since the end of his treatments. Returning to that state of helplessness was somewhat humiliating, but at this point, he was too tired to care. "Why don't you call the lodge and ask someone to bring it over?"

"You're right. I shouldn't leave you alone right now."

"That's not what I—" he started, but she had charged out the door. ICU nurse with a mission all the way. He smiled. But he supposed that was why she was as successful, and as fatigued, as she was.

God, he hurt. He felt as if someone had taken a hammer and beaten him with it. Each sting site throbbed laser beams through his body. His injuries were nothing like Skinny's though, and he couldn't imagine how much pain the man had been in. Reaching behind his head, he grabbed hold of the neck of his T-shirt and dragged it off over his head. Then he put a foot up on the toilet seat and untied one shoe, then the other.

A soft knock on the door interrupted him. "Mark? Are you in the tub? I have the baking soda. Do you want me to hand it to you or put it in the tub for you?"

"I think you're going to have to help."

Ellie pushed the door open and entered the room.

Sweat broke out on his forehead and chest and a chill soon followed it. Not good.

Ellie pressed her hand to his forehead and gave a small gasp. "You're hot."

"Cold, too." Taking a deep breath, he struggled to maintain his control. "Get me a couple of Benadryl, Tylenol and a shot of whiskey."

"Okay. I get the meds, but what will the whiskey do?"

"Settle my nerves or intoxicate me. I'm not sure which at this point." And right now, he didn't much care.

"I have something better than that. Let's just get you into the tub first, then I'll get the meds."

Mark let out a long sigh. "This wasn't how I had planned to spend the afternoon."

"I know. Me, either. How about you just let someone help you for a change, eh? As medical people, we're really bad about letting others help us, aren't we?" She continued speaking in a soothing voice as she helped him to undress. Grabbing a towel hanging on the rack, she covered his waist. "Let's maintain some privacy and cover your…stuff." Averting her gaze, Ellie blushed prettily, and Mark smiled at that.

"Sure. Like you haven't seen a man's stuff before." He was certain the towel was more for her modesty than his.

"True. Just not *your* stuff. And if we're going to work together the rest of the summer without being uncomfortable around each other, it's better this way."

"Agreed." Easing into the tub was no simple task while keeping the towel intact. "I feel like someone beat me up after pulling an all-nighter."

"You look like it, too." Leaning over him as she helped him ease down into the water, her clean fragrance and the scent of lavender passed over him. Unable to enjoy it due to the next wave of chill that hit him, he regretted that he was not in the tub with her under different circumstances. Any intimacy in his life was a distant memory. He didn't know about Ellie's love life. Unfortunately, the pain of the stings took his mind from going that direction at the moment.

"I can't believe what you just did," Ellie said and knelt beside the tub, shaking her head. "I've never seen anything like it." She dumped the entire box of baking soda into the tub and turned off the taps. With her hand, she swirled the powder so that it dispersed in the water. "Have you ever done anything like that before?"

Mark looked into her eyes as she paused. Something brief and electric passed between them before she dropped her gaze and picked up a washcloth. "No. I don't normally go out of my way to commit heroic acts."

"Yet you just grabbed the fire extinguisher and ran."

"I did something else first," he said, wishing he had the courage to try it again. Looking at her so close, maybe he did.

"Well, sure. You had to protect yourself with the bag over your head. It was a brilliant idea." She gave a nervous snort and her amused gaze met and held his. "I wasn't sure what you were doing at first though."

Mark raised his hand from the water, cupped the back of her neck and pulled her closer. "I meant this." And he kissed her. With her off balance in a kneeling position, he had no trouble pulling her the rest of the way to meet his mouth. Entirely too long had passed since he'd really kissed a woman, and he hungered for Ellie now. Her sweetness, her caring—everything about her pulled him in. For a moment, he needed to be just a man, in a tub, with a woman.

Soft and pliant, she opened her mouth to his. She reached across him and braced a hand on the other side of the tub. Imprisoning her face between his wet hands, he breathed in her scent, her warmth, and plundered her mouth with his lips and tongue. She tasted so sweet, felt so tender. Passion as he hadn't experienced since his illness filled him. He was in danger of revealing too much of himself physically and emotionally in the kiss. He eased back from her before he lost all control of the situation, and he was suddenly grateful for the position of the towel. His stuff had come to life.

Startled brown eyes peered at him. "Wow. What was that for?"

Smiling, he pressed his forehead to hers and caught his breath. "Because you're sweet, and I wanted to see if I remembered right."

"Right about what?" Returning to her previous position kneeling by the tub, she created some space between them.

"That your mouth was as soft as I remembered. I couldn't tell through the plastic bag." Was he out of his mind even contemplating getting involved with a woman, even on a temporary basis? A shiver claimed his attention away from making any decisions at the moment.

"You shouldn't be trying to jog your memory right now. Not when you're in this condition." She returned to nurse mode and placed the washcloth in his hand. "Keep washing this over you, and I'll go get those meds."

The phone in the main room rang, and she hurried out to answer it.

Amazingly enough, the baking soda trick seemed to be doing the job. The pain of the stings had begun to ease. He'd have to look more closely at home remedies for the simple things in the future. Minutes later, a gentle knock at the door announced Ellie's return.

"I've got the meds and some water." She handed him

the items and sat on the floor beside the tub. "Are you doing any better?"

After downing the pills, he closed his eyes and leaned his head back against the tub. "Yeah. Your remedy is working."

"I'm sure the medications will, too, but when you're out of the tub I'd like to use some oils on you."

"Sounds interesting. The purple oil or what?" He opened his eyes to slits to watch her. At the moment, that's all the exertion he could cope with.

"Yeah, the purple oil." She raised a large amber bottle of whiskey. "If you take this with the Benadryl, you'll probably fall asleep."

"Sounds okay to me." Although he hoped he hadn't made her uncomfortable with the kiss, he didn't regret it, either. Her lips were as soft as they appeared to be, and he liked the feel of them against his. "Why don't I get out, get some clothes on and then you can do the purple oil?"

"It's actually lavender oil."

"I know, but men only recognize primary colors."

"What?" Confusion appeared on her face. "That's not true."

"If you ask a man what color something is, he generally will tell you one of the primary colors. If you ask a woman what color something is, you're likely to get a description of something else, like lavender, or fuchsia, or chartreuse. I don't even know what color chartreuse is."

Ellie laughed, and the sound filled him with joy. This was the first time he'd heard such unadulterated laughter from her, and it was a good sound.

"That's absurd. Men see in more than primary colors—they simply refuse to acknowledge it."

"Not in my world, babe."

"That's so lame." She stood. "Anyway, can you get out and dressed by yourself?"

"Yeah. Just leave me a clean towel, and I'll make it." Weakness hadn't gotten him through all of the ordeals he'd suffered in the past few years. Leaning on Ellie for a moment had been nice, but he had to find his own inner strength again to finish the job.

"Okay. Just call if you need me." Rising, she moved away from him toward the door, then paused. "By the way, that was the hospital, and they're keeping Skinny in the ICU overnight. He's being intubated as a precaution due to the amount of stings he had on his throat and head, but he's at least responding well to treatment."

"Good to hear."

"Okay. I'll leave you to it."

Ellie left the bathroom and busied herself restocking the emergency kit and tried not to think of what had happened in the bathroom. The kiss.

Mark had *kissed* her. Again!

Why had he kissed her?

Why had *she* kissed him back?

Why was her heart *still* unsteady?

It wasn't as if she hadn't been kissed before. She certainly had. Mark had also given her a tiny kiss after pizza the other night. This kiss had taken her breath away, and she'd felt it to the bottom of her toes.

The door to the bathroom opened, and she heard

Mark slowly move down the hall to his room. She'd better get the oils ready. Fumbling with unzipping the pack she kept her oils in, she pulled out her favorite healing ones—rosemary, grapefruit and lavender. The grape-seed oil was in another bottle that nearly slipped from her fingers.

Come on, Ellie. You're a nurse. There's nothing special going on between you and Mark. You're just going to treat his injuries and go on with your life, right? Right. But the second that he entered the treatment room with her, she knew her little pep talk was a complete farce. She swallowed down the lump of desire that wanted to crawl up her throat.

Relying on her professional demeanor had gotten her through many difficult situations in the past, and she clung to it now as the only lifeline in the vicinity. "Moving kinda slow, huh?" She held out a chair and indicated he should sit.

"Being a human pincushion will do that to a man," he said and eased into the chair. "So what are you going to do?"

"I thought I'd start at the top, and work my way down. The first application of oils will be lavender, directly applied to the skin, then I'll do a mixture of a few others with some grape-seed oil." She stood upright, explaining the procedure as if he were a patient. There was no harm in that. Treat him just like everyone else.

"I see. Come a little closer, please." He motioned her forward.

CHAPTER EIGHT

COMPLYING, she picked up her bottle of lavender and moved closer. "Ready to get started?"

Without answering her, he reached out and clasped her behind the neck, pulled her closer and gave her a hard kiss.

Again! "What's with the kissing today?" Not that she didn't like kisses, but something was going on.

"I'm going to do that every time you hide." Green eyes bored into hers, challenged her.

"I'm not hiding," she denied and pulled away from him, gripping the bottle of oil tight in her fist. Seething anger burst through her.

"You are. You've got to be more than your job, or life is going to go flashing right by you. Since we've been here, I've only heard you laugh spontaneously once or twice, and rarely seen you do something just for fun, other than read, and you usually read aromatherapy books." He watched her, his playful mood giving way to a more serious undercurrent. "Why not relax a little, give yourself a break from whatever's bugging you?"

"Nothing's bugging me," she said and tried to find a way to deny the truth in his observations, but couldn't.

"Yeah, right. Ellie, every time something comes up where there's an opportunity to share of yourself or jump into an event with the others, you run the other direction."

She gasped, horrified. "I'm a Mackenzie. I don't *run* from anything."

"I know you value your privacy, but if something's bothering you, I can listen. I can be a sounding board if you need a problem solved."

"I don't have any problems." No, they'd all gone away when her fiancé had left her, and her dad had died. At least, that's what she kept telling herself.

"Ellie, we all have problems."

"Like you know anything about that." Highly irritated without a logical good reason why, she faced him. She opened the bottle and released the lavender fragrance into the room. "I'm sure everything came easily to you, didn't it? Probably went to an Ivy League undergrad school, took European vacations, sailed through medical school, didn't you?" She avoided his gaze and concentrated on dabbing the oil on her fingers, then applying it to the red welts on his shoulders and arms. "Despite the recent illness you mentioned, I'm sure your life has been a piece of cake compared to what I've been through in the past few years. You're too damned happy for it to have been otherwise, so don't tell me about watching life pass you by when you hardly know what it's like, Dr. Perfect." She said it as if it was a character flaw. Why, she didn't know, and didn't want to think about the knot in her gut as the words came out of her mouth. That was so unlike her, so totally uncharitable, but something snapped in her. "You have no idea what it's like to suffer."

He didn't deny or confirm her observations. Mark grabbed her hand and stopped her from her task, holding onto her until she looked at him.

Finally, she met his gaze, nearly trembling with emotion that she had denied lived in her. "What?"

"There's one more thing I am."

"What, football captain? Rugby captain? Debate team captain?" She meant to hurt him. She couldn't stop herself from doing it. The intensity, the look, in his eyes was what stopped her, and she paused in her emotional tirade.

"Cancer survivor."

The shock of his statement nearly drove her to her knees. "What?" she whispered and clutched his hand, despair and humiliation washing through her. Oh, God, she was so stupid.

"I'm a cancer survivor," he said and released her hand. "So I *do* know what it's like to see your life passing you by. Every damned day." His voice was gruff, and he closed his eyes for a moment.

Tears filled her eyes, pain for him shot through her and she closed her eyes to hide her shame. "I'm so sorry, Mark. I didn't know." She knelt beside him and sat back on her heels, her head lowered. "I don't know what's coming out of my mouth sometimes." She covered her face with her hands, unable to look up at him and see the hurt in his face that she had caused. "I'm sorry. It goes against everything that I am to be this way. I just didn't know."

"I know you didn't know. I asked Vicki and Sam not to tell you."

The sound of his soft voice, the forgiveness already there, made her want to weep, and she looked up at him, seeing the strength he'd had to find in himself. Reaching out, he eased her hands away from her face, then drew a line with one finger down her cheek.

"But why? I would never have said those things had I known." Tears leaked from the outer corners of her eyes, and she tried to brush them away on her shoulders.

"So you wouldn't treat me like a patient. Since surviving, I find that when people know of my history ahead of time they treat me differently than people who don't know." He shrugged and brushed away another tear with his thumb. "To them, I'm just a regular guy, and I like it that way."

Biting her lip, she hesitated, then blew out a long breath as she gathered her courage. "I'm sorry, Mark. Can I ask how you are doing now?"

"Yeah. I'm about three years out from the last clean CAT scan." He patted her hand and urged her up from her kneeling position. "Keep going with the oil. It feels good."

"Okay." Now, she would do anything to make him feel better, even if it was only a small physical comfort. She could never make up for the harsh words she'd spoken, but she could sooth his troubled flesh. She stood and continued to dab and apply the oil to the multitude of welts across his back, chest, arms and legs. "Thankfully, you were smart enough to do the bag trick. I don't know what would have happened to you had you been more exposed. Those little beasties are evil."

"No. I'm sure they were just protecting their nest. Some hornets nest in the ground, and Skinny may have simply stepped on one." He sighed and his eyes drooped a little.

"After I dose you up, I'd like to call the hospital and check on him again. Check on Bear, too."

"Sounds good." Mark stifled a huge yawn. "Wow. Looks like the Benadryl is kicking in."

"Didn't even need the whiskey. Why don't you go lie down in the ward room, and I can finish applying the rest of the oils to your legs and back there?"

Nodding, Mark stood and moved to the ward room and crawled facedown onto the nearest bed. "Man, I'm tired."

"It's been quite a day, hasn't it?" she asked.

Chuckling into the pillow, he then turned his head to the side. "Understatement of the year, I think."

"Between the meds and the oils, I think you're going to pass out here in a few minutes."

Another yawn claimed him, and he nodded. "Your powers of observation are astute."

"That's why they pay me the big bucks. One of the best skills a nurse can have is observation." Glad to see that he was truly feeling better and not upset about her comments, a warm glow began in her chest. Her touch and the oils were going to finish the job in just a few moments.

His words—*cancer survivor*—echoed in her mind.

He knew what it was to suffer, and he'd survived. There was no greater achievement in her eyes.

Mark allowed sleep to claim him. Undeterred by his lack of consciousness, Ellie continued to minister to his wounds. Actually, now that he was asleep, she felt freer to explore his body with her hands, to satisfy her need to touch him, to soothe him and to bring him a comfort that she wouldn't have been able to do otherwise. After the lavender, she poured her special mix of healing oils into the palm of one hand, then rubbed her hands together to warm the oil. Starting at his feet hanging over the edge of the bunk, she took her time and rubbed the oil into his skin, noting old scars here and there from minor injuries. She saw no surgical scars and concluded that they must be on his abdomen, and she'd simply missed them. Astute observation skills, eh?

His skin quickly absorbed the healing oils, and she moved upward over his calves, thighs, then his back and arms. Each touch, each stroke of her hand, she infused with her own healing energy that she hoped would bring him comfort.

"Ellie, you ought to consider massage therapy," Mark mumbled. "This is incredible."

She bit back the startled gasp that wanted to escape. "I thought you were asleep." She'd hoped he'd been asleep and hadn't heard her words of whispered sympathy.

"I'm kind of in a waking coma right now."

She smiled at that, knowing exactly how that felt after an aromatherapy treatment. Stress was nowhere to be found at that point. "Turn over, and I'll do the welts on the front."

"I'm not sure if I can move." But he turned slowly and collapsed onto his back. With a sigh of contentment, he closed his eyes again. "Go to work, Nurse."

"Yes, Doctor." She poured and warmed more oil and started again at his feet, working her way up. Though underweight a little, he had a beautiful body, and his muscles were toned and well formed. As she reached the top of his chest and neck, she found that her hands trembled as she stroked his skin. He opened his eyes, and she caught her breath at the heat in his gaze. Yet he didn't move. He waited for her.

Her mouth went dry, and she tried to swallow. Unable to look away from the need in his gaze, she froze. She hadn't allowed a man into her life for a long time. She'd been too caught up in helping her parents with her father's illness. Not that she hadn't dated on occasion, but Mark was right. She'd been watching life pass her by, and she hadn't even been aware of it. Did she dare try to stop and savor the moment presented to her right now?

Dropping her gaze to his mouth, some feminine instinct parted her lips. "Mark?" She didn't know what she was asking him. The question wasn't clear in her mind, and she didn't know how to translate that to him.

"Yes." He swallowed and raised his hands to cup her neck, drawing her slightly toward him. "Whatever it is, the answer is yes."

Unable to resist the draw of him, the pull of her heart toward him, she let herself go, and lowered her mouth to his. Though he'd kissed her earlier, this contact was completely different. This was need like she'd never known and it drew on her own suppressed needs.

He devoured her. Parting her unresisting lips, he drew her tongue into his mouth. Unable to suppress the heat of desire that gripped her, the glide of his tongue against hers tightened the knot in her stomach. Lord, the man knew how to kiss. Tremors that started somewhere in her middle spread through her body. Turning her head to the side, she parted her lips more and gave herself to Mark's heat.

Struggling to control the reaction of his body, Mark dragged Ellie against his chest and groaned. The feel of her weight against him, the taste of her sweetness and the fragrances mingling between them drew on every sense he had. For the moment, time ceased to move.

Ellie relaxed against him, and he savored every movement she made. She was lovely and caring, and he wanted to know her more than he'd suspected when they'd met. After thoroughly exploring her mouth, he released her and eased her upright.

She took in deep breaths, as did he. With one hand, he brushed her bangs back from her face. He liked her face and the animation she allowed to show now and then. There were mysteries and secrets hidden inside Ellie, and he wanted to discover what they were.

"Wow." She sat on the edge of the bunk beside him, and he was pleased that she didn't move away. One of her hands rested on his chest, and he liked the contact.

"Wow is right," he said. There was spark and chemistry between them, but he knew it took more than that to have a relationship that meant something. "Another surprise in a day full of them."

"Yes. Well." She glanced away, the movements of her hands busy and nervous now. "I have evening clinic in a little while. Dinner's in a few minutes, but I'm sure you'd rather stay here and rest." Reaching behind him, she straightened his pillow, and avoided his gaze. Back to nurse mode again. "I'll see if Bear can make a tray for you."

"Just a sandwich or two will work. Don't go to much trouble. I'll probably just sleep an hour or two."

Nodding, she rose, but he took her hand before she could get too far away. The medications and the events of the day were taking their toll on him, and he struggled to stay awake. "Will you stay with me tonight? In the ward room, I mean?"

"Yes. I'll stay." She brushed her hand over his face. "Go to sleep for a while now though. I'll be back in a bit." She moved to the foot of the bed and pulled a sheet up over him, then untucked it at the bottom. Leaning over, she kissed his forehead, then left the room.

A few hours later, after dinner and the clinic, Ellie reentered the ward room. Mark had adjusted his position and lay more on his right side, facing the doorway. His breathing came slow and deep, and she hoped the sleep was restorative for him.

Easing a bed closer to his, she tried to make as little noise as possible, but the feet of the bunk screeched across the wooden floor. "Darn it," she whispered.

Mark shifted and opened his eyes a crack. "Hi."

"Hi. I'm sorry I woke you." She leaned over and touched the back of her hand to his neck, then his forehead. He felt okay. "How are you doing? Did the sleep help?"

"Yeah. Yeah." He stretched and then took her hand. "What time is it?"

"About ten."

"I've slept for six hours?" he asked, his voice husky with sleep.

"Yeah."

"And you let me, didn't you?"

"Yeah, I did. You needed it. I'm still having waking nightmares about hornets, and I'm frankly not sure I'll be able to sleep tonight." She shivered.

"Don't worry. It's over, and everyone's okay." Mark rose and scrubbed his face with his hands. "I'll be back in a few." He allowed his fingers to trail down her arm as he left the room. Returning in a few minutes, he had foraged in the kitchen and found the sandwiches that Bear had sent, and a two-liter bottle of soda.

Ellie settled down on her bunk with one of her books and watched as Mark plowed through the food and downed the entire bottle of soda.

"That was fast. Are you going to need an antacid now?" she asked and parked her reading glasses on her nose, then turned on her book light.

"Nope. There are times when my appetite goes from zero to ravenous in a nanosecond, and this was one of those times. My metabolism kicks into overdrive." He patted his stomach and lay back on the bed; a contented sigh rolled out of him.

Though he had kissed her a couple of times, and she had offered him the comfort of her touch and healing oils, she didn't quite know what was really going on between them. Though they lived and worked together, she really couldn't say they were dating, and he'd not yet asked her out. This was a strange situation. Focusing on her book, she tried to see the print in front of her, but she'd read the same passage three times already and sighed, trying to remember what oil went with what.

"What are you thinking so hard about over there?" Mark asked.

Ellie looked up. Mark hadn't changed positions and remained with his eyes closed. "What makes you think I'm thinking hard about something?" she asked.

"I know the sounds of a female with something on her mind," he said and opened his eyes to peer at her in the near dark. "I grew up with three sisters. I know how the female mind operates."

"Ha," she said and snapped her book closed. "Did your sisters ever tell you that?" Secretly she smiled, but kept her face neutral.

"Hardly. They're too sneaky for that." Turning onto his side, he faced her and she put her book down. "Is there something you want to talk about?"

"Aside from hornets?"

"Aside from hornets." The bunks were just inches apart and he reached out to take her hand.

Looking down at the way their fingers intertwined,

she wondered if that was how people's lives intersected. So far she'd been too preoccupied with school, work and helping her parents that she hadn't been entwined with anyone since Alan. Had she gone too far to be able to find her way back? To be able to truly reach out for another and risk getting hurt? "I'm sorry, Mark. I should go back to my room. I don't want to keep you up."

"No, you shouldn't. I'd like you to stay with me here tonight. Will you?" He squeezed her hand, and his eyes drifted down again. The effects of the medications and the stings still remained in his system. She thought of offering him another aromatherapy treatment, but decided that sleep would probably be the best thing for him.

"I will."

He brought her hand to his mouth and kissed her knuckles. What a sweet gesture. She closed her eyes and listened to him breathing. The sound comforted her in a way she didn't know was possible. She extracted her hand from his grasp without waking him and covered him with a sheet.

In the darkness, she listened to the sounds of the night and wondered if she were already falling for a man she barely knew.

CHAPTER NINE

ELLIE woke the next morning to find Mark already up, showered and ready for the clinic. The horrors of the previous day had been slow to leave her brain. Every noise in the ward room had startled her subconscious until the wee hours of the morning, preventing her from having a good sleep. A yawn, a stretch; she rose and staggered to the coffeepot in the kitchen. Filling a ceramic mug, she took it with her into the shower and let the water pound her brain awake.

Mark stood in the doorway of the kitchen as she left the bathroom. The way he looked at her made her breath pause. He was so vibrant and alive in that moment. The welts had faded to pink overnight, and she almost didn't notice them. Then he smiled, and her heart fluttered erratically in her chest. She knew that a man like Mark couldn't go for a woman like her. Not long-term. She was too shy, too focused on her work, too ordinary to really attract him. At least, that's what Alan had told her over and over. Sure, while she was right under Mark's nose he was interested, but the second their ways parted, she'd be just an addendum to his summer in Maine. And she didn't want that. Couldn't handle it. What she wanted, and what she needed, was what her parents had had together. She glanced at the photo of them on the worktable. She'd settle for nothing less than that.

"I called and checked on Skinny."

"Oh, how is he?" she asked and stepped forward, then paused as a small herd of about fifteen children roared into the infirmary.

"I'll tell you right after clinic," he said and looked at the group of kids. "Now who's first?"

All of them shouted, "Me!"

Despite waking up on the tired side, Ellie had to laugh. The sight of Mark surrounded by the squealing children all vying for his attention was something to see. His laughter overrode the noise of the kids. When he looked over their heads and his gaze locked on hers, something in her heart cramped. "I gotta go." Before she could give herself a chance to fall into the trap of his green, green eyes, she turned and fled to her room.

Frowning, Mark watched Ellie rush down the hall. "What was that about?" he mumbled aloud.

"Dr. Mark, I need my inhaler," one child said with an audible wheeze that captured his attention. "I'm Tommy Brooks."

"You sure do." Each child had a medication file of their own. Mark reached in to Tommy's file and extracted the requested rescue inhaler and shook it. "One puff, wait a few seconds, then the other, okay?"

"I know. I'm not a kid," Tommy said with a roll of his eyes.

"You're right. Go for it." Mark tried not to laugh at the expression on the boy's face.

Tommy raised the device to his mouth and administered the medication as instructed.

Mark finished the short morning clinic, then knocked on Ellie's door. "Are you okay?" he asked.

With a smile that looked artificial, she opened the door. The glance she darted at him didn't meet his gaze. "Sure. I'm fine. Just didn't sleep well last night."

"Did I snore or something?" he asked, hoping he hadn't talked in his sleep. Who knew what secrets a man could reveal under the influence of Benadryl and aromatherapy? Now he was glad he hadn't added the whiskey on top of that.

"No. It's okay." She left the room with her pack of aromatherapy bottles in her hand. "I think I'm going to do a treatment on myself. I'm still a little freaked out by yesterday." She looked up at him and her face brightened. "Oh, you said you had a report on Skinny."

"Yeah," Mark said and followed her to the common room. "He's off the ventilator, breathing well on his own and out of ICU. Should be out of the hospital in a day or two."

"That's great news. Does Bear know?"

"He's the one who told me. He must have been over at the hospital at dawn." Mark wanted to reach out and ease the vulnerability and skittishness that he saw in her today, but thought better of it. Maybe it was just having spent an ill night that made her so jumpy. He hoped so. He hoped that the intimacy of helping him yesterday hadn't interfered in their professional relationship or the friendship he was beginning to enjoy with her. Though he knew he couldn't truly reach out to her the way he would have wanted to had circumstances been different, something about her continued to attract him. Clenching his fists, he resisted the urge that tried to draw him closer to her.

"I'm glad he's doing better." For a second she held his gaze, then dropped it to refocus on the pack in her hand. "I'm going to use the ward room to do an inhalation treatment on myself."

"I'll clear out, then, and give you a bit of privacy." This was the best way. They could work together, but not get too close. He could take the hint that she was obviously uncomfortable in saying it out loud, but her body language spoke the same message if he'd only open his eyes and put his libido on ice.

"It's nothing special, just a few oils that stimulate energy and pull the cobwebs out of my brain."

"I wish I had had that in medical school," he said.

She stepped back without comment and entered the ward room, then closed the door. Somehow the room had turned into their private living area when there were no patients in it. With a sigh he decided to have his run now before the heat of the day peaked. Summer was full upon Camp Wild Pines, and his time there was nearly half over. With a quick glance at the ward room door, he sighed, grabbed his ball cap and a bottle of water and headed out.

* * *

Refreshed after her aromatherapy session, Ellie sailed through lunch and the afternoon clinic, energy in every movement. With afternoon as the quiet time coming up, she was going to take the opportunity to catch up on her e-mails that she missed yesterday and drop a line to her mother. Several days had passed since she'd e-mailed her, and Ellie knew that her mother worried. Though her brothers were both in the same general area as their mother, they were married with kids and had busy lives that revolved around sports and summer activities for their kids. With a sigh, Ellie took her aromatherapy supplies back to her room.

When she returned, she stopped short and put her hands on her hips and looked down at the floor at an object that hadn't been there just moments ago. "Where did you come from?"

The little baby girl sitting on the floor looked up at her. "Ga?"

"Yeah, you." Ellie knelt down beside the baby when the screen door squeaked. She looked up, then screamed, "Vicki!" Ellie leaped to her feet to embrace her friend. "I can't believe you're here. Why didn't you call?"

The baby still on the floor gave a happy squeal and flailed her arms at the excitement in the room.

"Takes that surprise factor right out of it," Vicki said and pulled back from Ellie as Sam entered the infirmary. With another squeal the baby raised her arms to her daddy, who picked her up.

Vicki introduced Ellie to the little girl. "This is Myra. I know you've seen pictures, but this is the real thing."

Sam moved closer to Vicki, then leaned over and kissed Ellie's cheek. "Nice to see you again, Ellie." The baby wiggled to get down, and Sam returned her to the floor with a stuffed animal that she grabbed by the nose.

"Same here." Warmth filled her heart as she watched the family together. Joy mingled with a touch of envy in her heart. She was so happy that Vicki and Sam had worked things out between them, proving once again that good relationships could be had.

"Where's Mark?" Sam asked and eased his arm around Vicki's shoulders. Vicki looked up at him and the affection between them nearly filled the infirmary.

Ellie had to take half a step back, the energy nearly overwhelming her. "I'm not sure. Let me page him." She used the phone to access the camp intercom and asked Mark to return to the infirmary. "He's never far, so he should be here in a few minutes."

They chatted, and Ellie knelt to eye level with the blonde, curly haired girl. "She's just darling," Ellie said.

"Who's darling?" Mark asked as he entered the building from the side door.

Ellie looked up as Mark's long strides carried him closer to her. Seeing him so full of life and energy, vibrant and masculine, an overwhelming flood of attraction hit her. "What?"

"I said, 'Who's darling?'" He squatted down beside them. "This little one? Where'd she come from?"

"Right here," Sam said.

Surprise covered Mark's face and, for an instant, she saw the boy beneath the man. "Sam. Vicki." He charged forward and encased his friend in an exuberant hug. "Why didn't you call? We'd have made it a party."

"We can still make it a party," Vicki said and held her arms up for Mark's hug.

He kissed her cheek and gave her a squeeze. "Motherhood agrees with you. You look marvelous."

A quick flush colored Vicki's face, and she glanced at Sam. "I think you're right."

The group left the infirmary for a tour of the grounds, viewing the changes that continued to evolve since the fire two years ago. As they neared the wooded area beside the soccer field, Ellie noticed a patch of wild onions growing. She pointed to them. "Would you look at that?"

"Maybe that's why Bear's soups are so good. He's got his own private stash of wild herbs," Vicki said.

"Yeah, he mentioned something about you trying to weasel a recipe out of him." Myra wiggled in Ellie's arms and held her hands out to her mother.

"It took years, but I finally got it," Vicki said with a grin and took Myra back.

"What happened to you?" Sam asked and pointed to Mark's arms and legs and the fading welts. "Looks like someone mistook you for a pincushion."

"Hornets happened. Hospitalized Skinny yesterday."

"It was horrifying," Ellie said and told them how Mark had charged into the fray to save Skinny.

Vicki took one of Mark's arms and looked more closely at the marks. "What did you use on them?"

"Ellie fixed me up with some aromatherapy oils."

"In addition to some meds," Ellie added, not wanting to take credit for his entire healing process.

"I slept for twelve hours, and when I woke up they were like this, nearly gone."

"That's amazing," Vicki said. "I'm just glad you weren't hurt too badly." Vicki gave a full-body shudder.

"I did a lot of that yesterday," Ellie said. "I'm still a bit freaked out over it."

After the tour, they settled down at the lodge for a visit and to renew their friendships.

"I should go to the infirmary and put a note on the door, letting people know we're over here in case something comes up," Ellie said and stood.

"Good idea," Mark said.

"I'll be right back."

She left the lodge and placed the note, returning moments later to find Mark huddled in what appeared to be a serious conversation with Sam and Vicki. "You need to tell her," Vicki said in an urgent whisper. "There shouldn't be any secrets."

"I know. I know. It's not a topic that comes up in casual conversation though." Mark removed his cap and ran a hand through his hair, seeming more distressed than she'd ever seen him. If this was a private conversation, she didn't want to intrude. The three of them obviously had things to talk about that didn't include her, so she backed out of the lodge without letting the screen door make a sound and stayed on the porch a few more minutes.

Bear strode up the stairs to the lodge with a basket

of wild greens and a pair of kitchen shears in his hands. Now Ellie knew there were definitely some secrets in Bear's recipes.

"Hi, Bear, what do you have there?" she asked and tried to see into the basket.

"Oh, this and that. Some wild greens. Those fiddle-head ferns Skinny was looking for. Nothing special," he said and scooted around her, opened the door and entered. Ellie followed him inside and the trio broke up their conversation. Bear didn't slow down until he was safely tucked away in the galley.

"So what's the word?" Ellie asked, trying not to reveal that she'd heard part of the conversation. "Any plans while you're here?"

"I think we're going to let the men go have some catching-up time, and we'll do the same," Vicki said and held her hand out to Myra. "Let's go, girl."

"Mama, mama," she said and toddled her way through the lodge to the door.

After returning to the infirmary, Vicki settled Myra for a nap in the ward room, and they sat at the table in the kitchen.

"Last year we had part of the ward room turned into a nursery. She was just three months old, then."

"I'm glad things have worked out with you and Sam."

"So am I," Vicki said. "Though not without struggle, we finally found the place in our relationship where we could both be happy."

"Do you miss the ICU nursing?" Ellie asked and poured a glass of iced tea for each of them. If she didn't have her work, she didn't know what she would do. So much of her identity was wrapped up in her career, being a nurse, caring for others. If that was not in her life, it would be hard for her to imagine her life otherwise.

"No. Not a bit right now. My hands are full enough." Vicki raised her glass to her cheek and pressed it to her skin with a sigh. "This is lovely."

"I see." Ellie looked away.

"Are you missing the ICU already?" Vicki asked. "You can tell me."

"No. Not really." She looked around the small infirmary that had turned into her summer home. Moving from the ICU into a small building that had become the center of her life had been a drastic change.

"You sound surprised." Vicki sipped her drink, waiting for Ellie to reply.

"I guess I am. The chaos of the ICU is something I kind of got used to and didn't know until I left it how bad it really was for me, how overwhelming." Now that she said it aloud, she realized what a revelation that was. Her entire nursing life had been geared toward the high-tech side of saving patients. With that went high-level stress. And that wasn't what she wanted. She spent too much energy trying to de-stress, that she wondered if it was worth it. "Maybe I'm just not cut out for ICU work after all."

"It's amazing what taking a step back from things will do for you. I know the beginning of my nursing career was all about everyone else, and I nearly didn't have enough time or energy left for me." Compassion and understanding seemed to flow out of Vicki. She'd been where Ellie was now. She knew the difficult miles that Ellie had walked, and had walked many of her own.

Tears of unexpected grief burned Ellie's eyes. The pain in her chest came out of nowhere, and she leaned forward over the table. Vicki sat with her, not saying anything, but scooted closer and patted her back. The soothing gesture only made Ellie cry more.

Long minutes passed and so did the storm of tears. "I'm sorry, Vicki. I don't know what got into me." Wiping her eyes, she pulled herself together and took a few cleansing breaths.

"I don't, either, but it certainly wanted out." She patted Ellie again. "Do you feel better?"

"Marginally. I usually end up with a big fat headache after crying, so I really try not to do it." Crying just wasn't for her. She knew that some people derived great comfort from a good cry, but it had never worked for her.

"Then you need some other sort of emotional release."

"Definitely. Like what? At this point, I'm open to just about anything." Really. "As long as it doesn't involve sports."

Vicki thought a second, then her entire face brightened and her eyes twinkled. "I don't think it's really considered a sport, per se, but it might work for you."

"What? Tell me. I'll do it." Anything.

"How about sex?"

CHAPTER TEN

ELLIE burst out laughing. She'd never heard such a funny thing coming out of Vicki's mouth. But maybe that had been her intent. "Sex? *Sex*. What are you talking about? I haven't been in a relationship since Alan and, frankly, the thought of returning to him almost frightens me. Who am I supposed to have sex with, my imaginary lover?" She shook her head, totally dismissing the idea. That just wasn't going to work.

"How about Mark? He's available and right under your nose." Vicki watched her closely.

Narrowing her eyes at Vicki, Ellie sat back in the chair and crossed her arms. "Now I see what you're up to. This is a total matchmaking weekend for you, isn't it?" she asked and took a sip from her glass, eyeing Vicki over the rim. "Won't work."

"I really don't know what you're talking about, so what do you mean by that? Don't you find Mark interesting and attractive?" Vicki asked the question and somehow maintained a completely innocent look on her face. Oh, she was sneaky.

"Well, yes, of course," Ellie said and felt the burn of a blush begin in her chest and move up her neck. "He's very attractive. If you like that tall, lean, athletic stuff." She cleared her throat. "He's nice, too." She was going to get herself in trouble if she kept talking, so she clamped her mouth shut and looked at her friend.

"If you're looking uncomfortable and blushing, then something must be going on. Did he say he was attracted to you?"

"No. Not really." Ellie shrugged. "Though he did kiss me. A couple of times."

Vicki leaned forward across the table. "Aha. You don't call a kiss 'something'? What's it take to get your attention, woman?"

"I'm not sure anymore." Again, she shrugged, not certain of the point of this discussion since she and Mark would head their separate directions at the end of the summer, despite what could be called a mutual attraction going on. "After the first time, he apologized." That apology stung more than anything.

"But? There's more, I know it. I've known Mark for a long time, and he doesn't go around laying his lips on just anyone."

"Well, I said he sounded like he regretted touching me, but he said something I haven't quite figured out yet." She frowned as the memory of that tugged at her.

"What?"

"'Quite the contrary.'" Puzzled, she looked at Vicki. "What do you suppose he meant by that?"

"You *have* been out of it too long. It means he has

the hots for you, but respects you, too, and wouldn't jump your bones simply because you were convenient."

"Why do you think that is?"

The humor fled from Vicki's face. "He's been seriously ill."

"Yes, he told me a little about it."

"Did he tell you his fiancé left him in the early stages of his illness? In fact, during his first treatment."

Ellie gasped, horrified that someone would abandon their fiancé when they were needed the most. She would never do that. "No, and I'm not sure that you should be telling me, either. If he'd wanted me to know any more he would have told me." Though it felt like a violation of his privacy, she was glad to know a little more about him.

"I know. I know. He's a very private, very proud man. But he's also overprotective, way overprotective, of those he cares for."

"I'm not sure what you mean, but it's his life to live, isn't it?"

"Yes. Sam and I just want to see him happy and healthy, and part of that is having a good support system of loved ones around him." She sighed. "There's no more healing power in the universe than the power of love. But I'm not certain Mark can take that leap of faith and reach out for it after what he's been through."

"Now you're confusing me even more. Why wouldn't he be able to reach out to someone? He seems perfectly healthy now." He'd more than proved that yesterday.

"I don't mean to confuse you. The rest is for Mark to

tell you if he chooses. Just don't shy away from him if there's attraction between the two of you. It would be good for both of you." Looking around the infirmary, a dreamy smile came over her face. "There's something magical about this building, I swear. This was really where Sam and I worked out the problems between us, and where we fell in love all over again. Doing that a second time made us stronger together than we had ever been." This time tears made Vicki's eyes shine, and she waved them away. "Making me sentimental just being here."

"I think Bear is going to want to see you. He said he was going to miss not having you around here this year," Ellie said.

"He did? What a fooler he is. You just never know about that man." She shook her head. "As tough as he is, he's just a big old softy on the inside."

Ellie filled Vicki in about the grease burn and her use of aromatherapy oil on it. "You would have thought I dumped a bucket of perfume on him, the way he carried on about it."

Vicki laughed. "I can just see him now."

"He was really shook up about Skinny."

"They've been friends for a long time," Vicki told her, her eyes filled with concern.

"You should have seen Mark with that fire extinguisher. It was a brilliant idea, and I never would have thought of it. It was like watching something out of a horror movie." Ellie shivered as the memory of seeing both men covered in stinging insects hit her. "Still gives me the creeps."

"You were telling me Bear was pretty upset about the attack."

"Yeah. He went to the hospital this morning before Mark or I were even out of bed. Skinny's due back tomorrow, but he had a close call of it. Why don't you go over to the lodge and say hi? I'll watch Myra. She's sleeping, and I can handle her for a while."

"Good idea. I'll be back in just a bit." She rose and returned to the lodge to visit her old friend, Bear.

"Ellie?" Mark called as he entered through the side door into the infirmary. "Where are you?"

"In the ward room."

Again. It was definitely more comfortable than being in her cramped bedroom all of the time. He made his way down the hall and turned into the room, then felt as if someone had punched him in the gut. He stopped, because he couldn't move farther, and his breath froze in his lungs.

Eyes closed, humming softly, Ellie sat in a chair and rocked Myra, who was fast asleep on her shoulder. The sight almost made his knees go weak. Together, they were simply stunning. And something he wanted with every fiber in his soul. He didn't dare to try to make the dream a reality. Disappointment like that would destroy him.

Gathering his strength, he moved into the room and sat on the bunk nearest to them. Reaching out, he touched the small, perfectly shaped little foot with his finger. He was an uncle and had been around babies a lot, but the sight of such miniature perfection made him appreciative of the process of Mother Nature all over again.

Ellie opened her eyes and met his. The softness, the beauty in her face, made him want more than he knew he should. Wanting her, wanting a family of his own, was a dangerous undertaking when his illness could return at any time. That thought never left him.

"Is she asleep?" Ellie asked.

"Yes," he whispered and swallowed down the desperate needs trying to surface inside of him.

Ellie moved Myra and placed her back on the bunk, covering her with her light blanket. "Isn't she just beautiful?" Ellie asked, looking at the baby, then she looked up.

Holding her gaze, Mark had to agree. "Yes. She certainly is beautiful."

"You're not even looking at her." Ellie swallowed, and her gaze flashed to his mouth.

The tension between them was suddenly palpable, and he wanted to reach out to her more than he ever had. "That's okay. I see a beautiful babe right in front of me."

Ellie walked out of the ward room, and Mark followed her to the front. She turned to face him and opened her mouth to speak, but didn't have a chance to say a thing.

Mark was right behind her and stepped in close, cupped her face and kissed her. Hot and hungry for her, he gave her no options except to answer him with the same heat. Parting her lips, he delved his tongue and found her eager response. Oh, she was so sweet and pliant to his touch.

In an instant, his body hardened, ready to take this little embrace to its final fruition. Though his bodily functions had returned to normal since his illness, he hadn't tested himself yet with a woman, not wanting to fail her or himself. The humiliation and disappointment of being impotent after surviving his life-threatening ordeal was something he hadn't wanted to discover one way or another, but now, while folding Ellie into his arms, he was more motivated than ever to test himself. With her approval, of course.

Her approval came in the form of a throaty moan and melting softly against him. Not wanting to resist the sweet temptation of her, he knew he had to. So many conflicting emotions swirled inside of him, he couldn't make sense of any of them. And for the moment he didn't try. He simply enjoyed the sweet feel, the sweet taste, the sweet fragrance, of Ellie in his arms.

Finally, he lifted his head and pressed his forehead to hers as they caught their breath from the embrace that had taken them both by surprise. With his hands still cupped around her face, he held her softly. She was what he wanted, but his future was so unknown, so uncertain, that he knew he didn't have the right to want her so badly. She was backed up against the worktable, and he wanted to lie her down on it and strip her bare. The needs raging inside him nearly made him tremble.

Reaching up, she clasped her hands around his wrists and squeezed, though she didn't move away. "Wow. What was that for?" she asked.

"I don't know. I just needed it." And that was the base truth. He needed to be touched, to feel again, to express the emotions churning inside of him. Curving her hair back behind her ears he lifted his head, and she looked at him, cautious desire filling the depths of her eyes and her face. "Not that this is your problem, but I haven't made love since my illness." He smiled at the surprise on her face. "And to be brutally honest, Ellie, you're the first woman I've wanted to make love to since then."

"Oh." Her brows shot up. "Oh! Well, then." She dropped her gaze and started to move back from him.

"I've made you uncomfortable now, haven't I?" Damn. Sometimes he didn't know when to keep his mouth shut.

"No. Well, maybe a little." She fidgeted with the hem of her shirt and gave a nervous laugh.

"I'm sorry, Ellie. I just wanted to kiss you." Turning away, he ran a hand through his hair. "There's something going on between us. An attraction I hadn't looked for or expected to find. Especially not here at camp."

"Me, either. It's certainly surprising, but not unwelcome."

Dammit. He knew he should tell her the entire story, but somehow, in the speaking of it aloud, he almost gave life to the fears he didn't want to acknowledge. Vicki had said he should tell Ellie everything, but he didn't know if he should, wasn't sure he had the right words. What purpose would it serve if they were going to go their separate ways in a few more weeks?

"Mark?"

The sound of her soft voice made him turn back to her.

"There's more to your story than you've told me, isn't there?" She patted the worktable beside her and hopped onto it. Joining her there, he gave a deep sigh and decided to tell her the story that had been eating him alive inside.

"There's way more. So much more I'm afraid to say it out loud." His voice was rough with the emotions he'd tried to hide from her and from himself, but it obviously hadn't worked.

She took his hand and held it. "Why don't you just start talking, then stop when you're done?"

Compassion flowed from her into him, and he knew this was why she was such a good nurse, a good person, and needed this break from ICU nursing. She gave a lot of herself to others, but he didn't see that she was able to take much back from others who wanted to give a little to her.

"When I was diagnosed with testicular cancer just over three years ago, I thought for sure my life was over."

At her shocked gasp, he cringed inside. Maybe that wasn't the best way to say it, but he just had to tell his story. It was nearly alive inside him, clawing to get out.

"I'm sorry. Keep going." She squeezed his hand and urged him on.

"After diagnosis and surgery, I spent months in treatment hell. I developed a new appreciation for what our patients go through. There's no way to describe the experience, other than to say I survived it."

"Vicki did tell me that your fiancé bailed on you when you were sick."

"Yeah. She bailed all right. In the first week of treatment." He snorted and shook his head in disgust. "She couldn't bear being around 'all those sick people,' which included me."

"How selfish." Ellie clapped her hand over her mouth a second, then touched his arm. "I'm sorry. You must have loved her once."

"Not really. Amazingly enough, what I thought was love was somehow not. She was beautiful, but so shallow you could see right through her. For some reason I was looking for a woman who would make a good 'doctor's wife,' rather than looking for a friend and a life mate." He took a deep breath. "Having her take off really made me realize what was important in life and what was simply icing."

"Surely your family was with you through your treatment and recovery."

"Yes, they were. You mentioned your father died from cancer, so you know it's tough on a family, but it pulled us together, and we're closer than we ever were."

"Mom and I are much closer, too. So at least that's one good outcome from Dad's illness." She turned to face him. "So you told me that you've been clear of the disease for three years?

"That's right. Three years and counting."

"And you haven't found anyone of interest in that time?" The surprise in her eyes warmed him. "Seriously?"

"No." It was that simple. "Seriously." Until now at least.

"I find that hard to believe, Mark. You work with a lot of women in the hospital."

"Yep, I do. My sisters have even tried to fix me up with their friends, but there's just not been the right chemistry with anyone."

Silence hung between them. "You said you haven't made love, but have you...test-driven...yourself?" She clapped her hands over her face and turned a glorious shade of red. "I can't believe I just asked you that. I'm so sorry, don't answer that."

Mark chuckled, then a laugh, the likes of which he'd not felt in years, burst out of him. And he laughed until tears dribbled from his eyes. Off the table, he couldn't hold himself upright and he doubled over, laughing and laughing.

Ellie joined him. Reaching out, he hugged her to him, until the laughs subsided to small tremors that still shook him, and he had to sit down. "Yes, I have, so the parts work. However, taking my engine for a *test-drive*, as you say, and putting it through an *endurance race*, are two entirely different things."

"I suppose they are." She wiped away a tear from her face.

"The big issue, too, is that I don't know whether the sperm I make is viable." That was something he hadn't wanted to tackle yet, either. Somehow not knowing the answer to that was better than knowing he was infertile.

"You haven't done testing since the treatment?"

"No." He shrugged, the humor of the moment beginning to fade. "I haven't wanted to find out. If I'm not in a serious relationship, what's the point?" And since he wasn't going to be in a serious relationship until he made it to his fifth cancer-free year, there was no point. Having the information wouldn't solve anything if he was still going to die.

"The knowing might bring you some peace of mind, don't you think? I don't know a lot about testicular cancer, but I've read that storing sperm before treatment can give you some hope for children later."

"If you survive the treatment and the first five years, you mean?" He squelched the bitterness that wanted to leap out of him. Sometimes the emotions of it all just got to him, though he tried not to let it take over his life.

"Well, yes."

"I did save sperm, but I always preferred doing things the old-fashioned way, especially when it comes to children. I'd rather not create my children in a lab if I don't have to." He shook his head and took in a breath, willing the pain of that thought to go away.

"That would probably be everyone's first choice. For some people, that's the only way they can have children."

"I know. I know. And it's a wonderful option, but at this point, for me, it's just moot, since there isn't a line of women beating down my door to marry me and bear my children, is there?" The last one had left him when he'd needed her the most, and he'd not wanted anyone in his life since then.

"Mark," she said, and he heard the reproof in her tone. "That's a nasty thing to say about yourself. There's a lot more to you than being a sperm donor and making babies. You could have a wonderful relationship with someone, even if you never had children."

"I know. I know. I didn't mean to unload my problems on to you, Ellie, I'm sorry." He ran a hand down her arm. "You've started to become a good friend, and I didn't need to do that to you." Irritated with himself, he started for the door, but her hand on his arm stopped him.

"You weren't unloading problems, Mark. And you *are* starting to be a good friend. Until that last crack, we were good."

Anger in her face and eyes surprised him. He hadn't expected that. "But?"

"Friends share things, and you don't need to police what you say to me."

The compassion, the interest, in her eyes nearly made him want to reach out to her in a way he hadn't allowed himself to reach out for years. But something stopped him. "There are just some things that you don't need to hear. That's all." Some things he could hardly stand to hear himself.

"Mark! Just stop it, will you? Have you listened to yourself? You sound like you're ninety-five years old and ready to give up."

"I can't help it, Ellie! Until you go through this experience yourself, face your own death, you can't know how deeply you're going to be affected." He was surprised at how emotional he'd gotten. Tremors of rage he thought he'd suppressed pulsed through him. Clenching his jaw tight for a moment, he refused to give in to the emotion of the moment.

"I understand that. I'm not saying that I know what

you're going through, or what you've been through, but I have suffered in ways that you don't know." Her voice cracked, and she cleared her throat. "I just want you to know that I can be here for you, that I can listen when you need to talk." Pausing, she knelt beside him and took his hands in hers, but she didn't look at him, keeping her gaze on their entwined hands. She pointed to her left ring finger. "There used to be an engagement ring on this finger." Her voice dropped to an emotional whisper.

"What happened?" Sick with anticipation, he gripped her hands in his, almost knowing what she was going to say. Now he knew he didn't have the right, shouldn't have the want, to desire her. She'd been through too much emotionally already, and he'd only give her more.

"The man I was to marry, to build a life with, wouldn't share me with my family. We had been together for years and had every intention of fulfilling the all-American dream."

Unable to resist, he reached out to stroke her hair. "And the dream faded?"

"More like it was shattered by a narcissistic idiot who thought the world revolved around him." Now, she looked up at him, the passion of righteous anger blazing from her eyes, and he almost pulled away from the intensity of her. "When I paid more attention to my father during his illness than Alan, he couldn't take it. He got pissy, then angry, then he sulked. Do you know that when a man sulks, it's a massive turnoff?"

Suppressing a grin, he said, "I'll try to remember that."

"Anyway, he never said it in so many words, but he

wanted me to choose between him and my dying father. Do you believe that one?" She stood and paced in front of him.

"Obviously, you chose your father."

She snorted. "Obviously. I figured if we were truly meant to be together he'd still be there after things settled down with Dad, but it didn't, and he wasn't."

"I'm sorry, Ellie," he said, and meant it. A bad heartbreak could scar a person for life.

"He made a promise to me, and he broke it. It's that simple." She turned to face him, giving him a stare that all nurses seemed to possess. "There are no guarantees in life, Mark. You know this. People say one thing and do another. They change, they change their minds, they simply just go away. You'd do well to reach out and embrace whatever you can in life, because you don't know how long it's going to be there. If you're waiting for some miracle woman to show up at the right moment in your life, you may be waiting a long time." She huffed out a sigh and seemed to withdraw into her own mind for a second. "I loved a man and lost him. Yes, it hurt, but I've moved on. I don't want to get hurt again, but we don't know what's around the next corner, or the next one, or the one after that. All we can do is reach out to what's right in front of us and hold on."

Cries from the ward room halted their conversation. Saved by the baby. "Guess this conversation is over." How could he tell her that he simply couldn't reach out the way she suggested? She'd been through enough pain in her life and though she said reaching out was the way to go, he didn't want to knowingly cause her pain.

Ellie moved toward Myra, then paused. "For now. But it's not over, Mark. We still have more than half the summer left."

Nodding, Mark left the confines of the infirmary, and wished he could leave his dark mood behind as easily.

CHAPTER ELEVEN

VICKI and Sam returned to the infirmary, collected the baby and headed to their hotel for the night. There simply wasn't enough room in the infirmary for all of them to stay comfortably. That was okay with Ellie. She liked her space as well as her friends.

The summer heat loaded with humidity had descended, and she couldn't sleep anyway. Pressure in the air seemed to force her muscles to work harder than usual to accomplish the same tasks. The air-conditioner unit in her room blasted away, but it was heated dreams and raw desires that kept her from falling into a deep sleep. Humidity was just an excuse.

Mark's touch, the scent of him, the taste of him and the feel of his body against hers, drove her to a state of restlessness that she hadn't anticipated. Desire was something she'd put on hold through her father's illness and now that she'd found some freedom outside of the hospital and the controlling relationship she'd had with Alan, it appeared that her body had also found the freedom it needed to respond as fully as it wanted to.

Dreams were hot and sweaty, with familiar bodies straining together, and she woke with a desperate need in her, a need that had been awakened and refused to go away. Mark was down the hall. He was the source of her current situation. He was also the solution.

Could she take that tiny step, that giant leap, toward him, to what he could offer her, even if it was only temporary? Didn't all relationships start out as temporary anyway? Who needed commitments or promises that were unwisely given in the heat of a moment, when the heat could change to ice in a millisecond?

She'd rather not have broken promises, only shared moments, between them.

Desperate to cool off and hose down the desire rumbling inside of her, she left her room and sought out a glass of ice water in the kitchen. That only succeeded in quenching her thirst; the heat of her inner turmoil persisted.

"Stop it!"

Ellie jumped and flashed around. "Mark?" She knew she'd heard his voice, but he wasn't behind her as she'd expected.

A muffled voice came from his room, and she hurried barefoot to him. "Mark?" She pushed the unlatched door wide and saw him fighting with his sheets. He had to be asleep, struggling with his dreams as she had been doing. Getting close to a thrashing person in the throes of a nightmare could be dangerous, as she'd experienced in her hospital work. So she called his name from the doorway.

"Mark? Wake up. Mark. Wake up."

At the sound of his name he stilled, his chest heaving. Though his eyes opened, she doubted that he was fully awake yet. "Mark, it's Ellie. You're having a dream."

"Oh, my God." He sat up on the edge of the bunk, rested his elbows on his legs and held his head in his hands. His breath wheezed in an out of his lungs as if he had just been running through the camp.

Sitting beside him, she placed a hand on his back. "Are you okay? Want a drink of water?" She handed him her glass and he drained the frigid water in seconds.

"Wow. Thanks." He tried to peer through the darkness at her, though with only the hallway light, she couldn't tell how much of her he saw. "What are you doing up? Did I wake you?"

"No. My own dreams woke me. I got up for water, then heard you."

"Sorry."

"Not your fault. The heat kept me from sleeping." At least that was a partial truth. "Want to talk about it?"

"I'll tell you my dream if you tell me yours." He pressed the glass still filled with ice against his cheek, trying to cool off.

"Uh, I'm not sure that's a wise idea." Really unwise if she intended to keep her secrets to herself.

"Why not? Didn't you just flay me on that point earlier tonight? It's just us, we're friends, it's the middle of the night and we're sitting here in the almost dark." He placed the glass on the floor. "There's no one except us, Ellie. Tell me about your dream. I want to hear about it to distract me from mine."

Oh, she knew she was going to regret this. "Okay." She huffed out a sigh. "I was dreaming about you. And me. About our conversation earlier tonight." The dark lent some sort of secrecy, some anonymity, though she knew exactly where she was and to whom she was talking.

"What about it? I really didn't mean to burden you with my problems."

Ha. "It was no burden at all. It was quite the opposite." She licked her lips, which had suddenly become dry. Hmm. Her throat was dry, too, though she'd just had some water. "It was exhilarating actually."

"I don't follow."

The darkness seemed to expand and fill her mind as she remembered. Images from her dream flashed through her mind; electricity zinged through her as desire began to once again unfold. "We were together in my dream."

"Together?"

She nodded, even though he couldn't see her. "And…naked."

"Aha. Now I see what kept you awake. You were taking me for that test-drive, weren't you?"

There was humor in his voice, and she responded to that. Laughter bubbled in Ellie, though she tried to hold it back. "Uh, yes. I was taking you for a test-drive."

"How was the engine performance?" he asked. Though she couldn't see him clearly, she felt him shift position to face her, but more than that, she sensed a shift in the air between them. She wasn't the only one who was affected by her dream. In telling Mark, he responded as she had in the dream.

"It was going well until I doused it with ice water."

"Ouch. That brought things to a halt, didn't it?"

She licked her lips, trying to find some of that moisture she'd recently downed. "Temporarily." She paused. "Until I came in here."

He huffed out a sigh and placed his hand on her arm, stroked it down to her hand. "You know I want to make love with you, Ellie. I'm not just saying that because you're here with me now, you know that, don't you?"

"Yes. I feel the same way. And it's not because of the dream, but it's because of who you are, and what you are, and everything, that I... God, this just isn't coming out right."

"What?"

"Will you hold me, Mark? Just for tonight, will you hold me?" Could it be as simple as that? Just two people holding each other in the dark and allowing the rest of the world to go away for a time.

"Ellie. Don't pity me because of what I told you. I couldn't handle that." His grip on her hand tightened.

She snorted. "Believe me, it's not pity that's pounding through me, Mark. It's pure, unadulterated lust."

"Oh, Ellie. You make it hard for a man to say no." His hand clenched hers and the tremors in him shot through her.

Reaching out into the dark she found his face and turned it to her. "Then don't say it." Moving closer, she pressed her cheek against him, rubbing, feeling the scrape of his overnight beard against her skin. "Please hold me, Mark. I need you to hold me." The world needed to go away just for a little while.

"I don't think holding you will be enough," he breathed and cupped her face in his hands. "At the moment, I can't muster the strength to resist you, resist what's going on between us." He turned his face toward her.

This was just where she wanted to be. "I'm not sure if I remember how to make love anymore, Mark. It's been so long." Desperate desire overwhelmed any self-doubt. She needed him.

"Try," he whispered against her lips.

Already charged up by the erotic dream she'd had, Mark's touch was magic, and ignited her in ways she'd never imagined. Each kiss, each stroke of his tongue against hers, each gentle press of his hands on her skin, stoked the fire higher. She wrapped her arms under his and cupped his back with her hands.

They lay back on the bed, and Mark shifted his position until their legs tangled together, his hips pressed against hers. Yes, his engine was definitely ready for high performance now. The heat of his arousal pressed hot and hard against her belly. With only a thin nightshirt that rode up high, she felt every inch of him through his boxers, and she suppressed the groan in her throat. Desire that had blossomed now surged in electrical pulses through her.

He kissed her cheek, her neck, and made his way down to tug at a nipple through the fabric, and she arched at the wet heat of his mouth. Reaching for the hem of the nightshirt, he tugged and pulled at it until it was up over her head, trapping her arms at her sides. "I want to touch you," she whispered. "My arms are stuck."

Without replying, he opened his mouth over her nipple and pulled it inside, and she forgot what it was that she was protesting. Surges of electricity shot through her, and her mind no longer functioned properly. This was definitely what they both needed.

Each stroke of his tongue on her tender flesh was an agony of the senses. Low in her belly, her flesh came alive. Surges of heat and moisture shot through her, quivers of desire made her gasp as he took her deeper than she'd ever been. The past had no place here.

Mark lifted his head and ringed his tongue around her other nipple while his hands got busy and tugged at the scrap of panty she wore and dragged it off of her.

Following his hands downward, he kissed the slight curve of her belly, the flare of her hips that his hands had itched to touch for days and days. Her skin was so soft, and she smelled of lavender and honey, and some essential feminine fragrance he knew he'd inspired in her.

"Mark, wait—" She breathed quickly, seeming to sense his destination.

"Shh. Shh. Easy, love." Urging her knees farther apart, he kissed her thigh and rested his face against her lean leg and sighed, totally content in this position and the moment between them. "You are so beautiful, Ellie. So beautiful."

Restless, her hips moved, and his mouth watered to taste her. Unable to deny himself any longer, he turned his face to her center and opened his mouth over her.

At the first touch of his mouth on her feminine flesh, Ellie cried out and stiffened, clutching the sheets in her fists. Then, her knees drifted slowly apart. Allowing himself to explore her soft body as he wished, he teased and tugged and stroked until her breathing hitched. Easing a finger inside of her heat, he took her over the edge. Her choked cries filled his ears; the spasms of her body let him know that he had satisfied her. Easing upward, he pressed a long hot kiss to her mouth, and she held tight to his face. Then he drew away.

Pulling himself upright, he fumbled around in his nightstand. "Where are those things?" he mumbled aloud, then he found what he was looking for.

"What?"

"I confiscated some condoms from a few of the older boys who were using them to make water balloons," he said and tore the box open, spilling them all over the place. Grabbing one, he opened it and brushed the rest to the floor.

"This is a much better use for them."

She reached for him and, with her hands assisting his, eased the condom over his erection. Her touch was magic, and he was rapidly losing any control he might have once claimed.

"Are you sure about this, Ellie?" he asked, hoping that he wouldn't fail her with the rest. Stopping now might render him incapable for life.

"Come here," she said and pulled him to her. With a groan, she found his mouth, and he lost himself to her eager touch. Kisses deep and hungry, her touch setting him on fire, he knew that this was what he wanted, what they both needed, and he raised himself above her, then paused.

The feel of her nails digging into his hips, urging him forward, gave him the last little bit of courage he needed, and he eased inside her moist sheath.

"Oh, Ellie." She was so soft, so hot, so incredibly firm around him, that he thought he might explode right there. But as his body seemed to remember what to do, he released the control of his mind to simply feel and enjoy Ellie's body as sensations took over. He knew that no matter what happened between them, he would never forget this night.

"Mark," Ellie cried as she clutched him closer, her breathing faster.

She tipped her hips up, and he surged into her. Sweat broke out on his skin as he pulled back, then moved forward, easing into her again. She wanted to please him as much as he seemed to want to please her.

Sighs and moans, and the sounds of flesh against flesh, filled the air between them. Sensing that Mark was close to a release, she wrapped her legs around his hips and pulled him hard into her, her fingers digging into his hips. Tension mounted as her body surprisingly prepared again for surrender, and she pressed her face against his moist neck. Holding him tight with her legs, and squeezing him with her arms, her body took over and tremors shook her.

An instant after the orgasm took hold of her, Mark trembled in her arms, and he cried out with the ferocity of his own release. Rocking back and forth with her, he drew out the pleasure for the both of them as long as possible, then he collapsed on top of her. His breath wheezed in and out of his lungs as heavily as it had the first day she'd met him.

Then he laughed and it was pure joy that came out of him. "Ellie. I think you remembered just fine." He pressed quick kisses all over her face that made her smile. Then he dove in for a long, hot kiss that ended with a gentle touch of his lips on hers. "You are so wonderful. Thank you, Ellie. You have no idea how much I needed this, how much I needed *you*." The trembling of his body told her how much.

Without moving, she held onto him. Now that she'd reached out to him, she didn't know if she wanted to let him go.

CHAPTER TWELVE

THE next morning there was absolutely no time to reflect on whether it was right or wrong that Ellie and Mark had made love, or if great sex was really one of life's ultimate stress busters.

Starting at the time her alarm went off, the infirmary was in crisis. Highly contagious stomach flu had hit the camp and left no cabin unaffected. At least three campers from every cabin went down at once. When those kids recovered, three more replaced them in the infirmary. Ellie dispensed all of the stomach medication that she had available and sent Gil to town for more.

"Here it is," he said as he charged through the door with several sacks of medication in his hands. He placed the bags filled with pink liquid medication on the worktable. "I went to the pharmacy and the store and bought every bottle they had. They'll have more tomorrow."

"Thanks, Gil." Exhausted, Ellie opened the bags, took out three bottles and handed them to Gil with a bottle of hand sanitizer. "Mark's out making rounds in the cabins, and I've got a ward room full, so I can't leave. Can you find him and give these to him?"

"Sure." He took the items from her.

"After that, wash your hands and lock yourself in your office if you can."

"Got it." He left and the phone rang.

"Infirmary from hell, Ellie speaking." It was Vicki. "We've got a massive case of stomach flu here, so you three ought to stay away for a few days." She sighed with regret. "That will probably be the end of your visit here, but I don't want you to get sick, too. This is awful." She'd lost track of how many kids came and went, how many brows she'd mopped and how many doses of medication she'd administered. Everything was beginning to take on the same pink hue.

"I'm so sorry. We wanted to spend some time with you and Mark, but we leave in two days."

"I'm not certain we'll be over the worst of this by then and it's not worth the risk, especially for Myra." From the looks of the ward room, the bug wasn't going to be over until it had infected every person in the camp.

"Is there anything you need me to bring? I can do a shopping trip for you and drop it off at the back door of the infirmary without risking exposure."

"Oh, Vicki. If you could get me a couple of things, I'd totally appreciate it." She gave Vicki a short list of necessary items. "You're such a good friend. You have no idea how much I need that right now." Tears nearly sprang to her eyes, but she resisted them. Fatigue was what was getting her down, and her emotions were just raw right now.

"I do know. I was having trouble myself a few years ago, remember? You helped me a lot by just listening, so now it's my turn to help you out. Just let me do this for you, will you?"

With a tired laugh, Ellie said, "Okay. I'll let you." She hung up and returned to the ward room to the sounds of renewed retching from one of the children.

"Oh, you poor little ones," Ellie said and emptied yet another emesis basin, then dosed the child with the pink stuff. She sat by his bedside stroking his hair until he drifted off to sleep. Washing her hands in between each bed, she moved on and on until she could hardly stand upright. The skin on her hands was raw and cracked from so many washings and applications of hand sanitizer. She'd definitely need some heavy-duty oils after the crisis was over.

A phone call from Vicki alerted her to the delivery of her supplies. Vicki had set three bags of items at the side door without Ellie even noticing that she had come and gone. She put away the perishables, then let the rest sit on the counter until she had time to deal with them. At this rate, camp might be over by the time that happened.

During the three days of exhausting, repetitious tasks, Ellie and Mark caught naps and showers and food when they could, spelling each other at intervals. Any discussion of what had occurred between them had had to wait.

The tidal wave of campers flowing in and out of the infirmary slowed down to a trickle, and Ellie collapsed facedown on a clean bed in the ward room. She'd scrubbed with soap and water, then applied anti-infective spray for good measure to each surface of every bunk, every door handle and all possible sources of contaminant. Fomites were not going to reinfect anyone if she had anything to say about it. She'd washed all of the sheets and put them back onto the clean bunks. Exhaustion nearly claimed her. There were now four potentially undisturbed hours between now and the next clinic, and she intended to sleep through every minute of them.

Groaning, she let out a long sigh and settled down for a nap. The scent of lavender oil soothed her fraught nerves and she breathed deeply, then frowned. Lavender oil? Where had that come from? Had she left a bottle open somewhere? She opened her eyes and saw Mark standing beside the bunk, her bottle of mixed aromatherapy oil in his hand. "What are you doing?" she asked and heard the fatigue in her own voice. If she could hear it, then obviously Mark could, too. Although he didn't look it, he couldn't be in much better shape than she was at the moment. She pushed her arms against the mattress and eased into a sitting position.

"You're exhausted, so I thought I'd give you some of your own medicine." He poured a dollop of oil into his hand. "Go back to the way you were, and I'll give you a purple treatment."

"Aren't you tired, too? You've been at this as long as I have." Although he looked a little rough around the edges, he didn't look nearly as bad as she felt.

"Yeah, but I had half a pot of coffee and a shower,

and I'm good for a while. Residency was good training for these past few days." He grinned and the light in his eyes darkened. "No worries. It's time you had a little relaxation time of your own instead of taking care of everyone else."

"Mark, no. It's really okay. You don't have to spend time on me when you should be resting, too." He wasn't going to do this. "It's an unnecessary use of your time when you don't have any more than I do."

"Ellie."

The drop in his voice made her pause and look up at him. "What?"

"Be quiet and lie down. Doctor's orders."

Resistance boiled strong inside of her. "But—"

"You're not being a very good nurse by disobeying doctor's orders. Why are you resisting me?"

"It's not you," she said and dropped her gaze, wondering when the pulse of anxiety within her was going to go away. They'd made love. It wasn't as if he hadn't ever touched her. He knew her intimately. "It's just not necessary. I don't need it."

"I most heartily disagree. You need this as much as the kids needed your touch, your calming influence that you don't even know you have. How are you supposed to fill up your soul if you don't stop every now and then to try? Giving of yourself so much has put you right where you are."

"Where, Maine?" The attempt at humor fell flat.

"No. The edge of exhaustion. And besides, I want to touch you the way you touched me. The way you helped me." He knelt beside her and placed his oily hands on her thighs. "Just breathe, Ellie. Just breathe."

The gentleness in his voice was nearly her undoing. She couldn't be weak, especially not in front of him. Tears spilled from her eyes. Where had those come from? She brushed them away. She didn't cry. Ever. Tears were an indulgence she couldn't afford. Unable to refute his claim, she remained silent. Unfortunately, he was right. "I just don't know how to allow myself to enjoy things like that anymore. Not since…well, not in a long time."

"Sure you do. Things you don't think are important for you really are. But I have to tell you from experience that the human touch, connecting with another person, is one of the things that got me through my illness."

"Which was so much more serious than my silly problems. What's a case of fatigue compared to a near-death experience?" It was nothing. She knew that. But the memory of his touch made her want to do exactly as he suggested and surrender to him, to give up the need to be strong all of the time. Honestly, she was simply too tired to fight anymore. A sigh rolled out of her, and the burning in her eyes made her close them for a second.

"Ellie, quit talking and lie down."

Unable to resist him or herself any longer, she gave in. Exhaustion made her weak and tears continued to dribble down her nose and wet the pillow under her head. "I'm sorry."

"That's it," he said in a soothing voice and touched her with his oil-soaked hands. "That's my girl. Quiet, slow breathing. Empty your mind. Close your eyes and just enjoy."

Strong and sure, his hands began the journey at her bare feet, applying the oil and massaging her tired muscles. She ached everywhere and a groan of pure bliss came out of her throat as he pressed his thumb firmly into the arch of one foot. "Oh, God, Mark. If I had *any* government secrets, I would give them away right now."

He chuckled. "Feel good, eh?"

"Beyond description," she said and allowed a long sigh to unfold from somewhere deep inside of her. "I feel so weak admitting that to you."

Moving up to her calves, he poured more oil into his hands and began to massage the stressed muscles there. "Why is it weak to admit you enjoy something? The human touch is very important in well-being. You've had a tough year. Being an ICU nurse is no easy thing, then to have your dad's illness piled on top of the fiancé rejection. That is beyond the ability of most people to sanely handle without needing some sort of break."

"Until the other night, with you, I haven't had the human touch, that intimacy, for a long, long time. Alan wasn't very demonstrative unless he wanted something. For him, intimacy was a means to an end, rather than something you do when you care about someone." Tears that she thought she'd finishing shedding began to fall again. Sniffing, she tried to hide her reaction from Mark and turned her face away. "I don't want to think about that part of my life anymore."

"I think you need the connection with others more than you realize or that you've allowed yourself to have." He soothed her with his touch and with his voice. "Don't be afraid to be vulnerable with me, Ellie. Don't be afraid to feel your emotions."

"I've had to be strong for so long, that I don't quite know how to do that."

"Just let go for a little while. Give yourself a break and lean on me for a little while. It'll be okay," he said and pressed a kiss to the back of her head. He straightened her arms by her sides, applied the oil, then stroked her back. No one had offered her such comfort since she'd been a child. After another breath filled with the healing fragrance of lavender, she finally gave in to the exhaustion that overwhelmed her.

Mark watched as she fell asleep, amazed at the personal strength and sheer stubbornness that had seen her through some troubled times. Though impressed by the things she'd accomplished, there was something else about Ellie that reached into his spirit and made him want to stay by her side for more than the rest of the summer.

She was lovely, and courageous, and strong, and before the end of the summer he was going to convince her of it. If he left her with nothing else, he would do that for her.

Voices alerted him to the arrival of a camper. He left the ward room to catch them before they woke Ellie.

CHAPTER THIRTEEN

NIGHT fell before Ellie woke. Unable to tell the time from the light, she entered the main room to find it empty and the clock reading well after clinic hours had ended. She'd missed it, and Mark apparently had handled it without her. The thought of that didn't disturb her as much as it had just a few weeks ago. Maybe she was learning to be more of a team member instead of being the entire team. That was just getting to be too much work.

The rustle of papers drew her to the screened porch. She stepped out, and Mark looked up. He wore reading glasses perched on his nose, a glass of water sat beside him on a small table and he was reading from a professional journal. The smile that lit up his face stopped her. He was simply the most wonderful man she'd ever known. He was kind, generous, sexy to a fault, had a sense of humor that she enjoyed and he didn't let her take herself too seriously. Had she fallen in love with him without even knowing it?

"Hi, there. Have a good rest?" He removed his glasses and tucked them into the collar of his shirt.

"The best in a long, long time." Admitting that wasn't as scary as it might have been a few weeks ago. Maybe she was finally healing from the rigors of her job and the lingering grief of the past year. Life moved on, and she had to move along with it.

"Must have been the aromatherapy oils. Good combination you made." He patted the seat beside him.

"Yes," she said and moved to the swing and sat with him. What would it be like to enjoy the same sort of relationship that Sam and Vicki did? They'd been through their tough times, and she knew every relationship had them. Finding the right person was something that happened to people, but so far hadn't happened to her. She'd begun to think that the relationship fairy had skipped over her. Perhaps that fairy had returned now with an unexpected gift. After Alan, she had some making up to do.

"Where are you?" he asked and closed the journal.

"What?" She blinked several times and peered at him. What had he said?

"I asked where you were," he said and tapped her temple with one finger. "You were miles away there for a minute."

"I think I was." There was no harm in admitting that, was there?

"There's something I want to ask you," he said and turned more closely to face her.

Without verbally answering, she raised her brows.

"The kids will be heading out for a long day trip in a few days."

"Yes, I know. It's going to be a project getting everything ready." She was just glad the medical team didn't have to go along. One whole day to themselves was going to be pure bliss.

"I was wondering if you'd consider going somewhere with me." He uncrossed, then recrossed, his legs and shuffled the magazines in his lap.

"Sure, where?"

"How about a date?" He hadn't really intended to ask her like that, but the second she appeared, warm and sleepy, on the threshold of the porch, he knew he'd had to ask. He wanted time with her, away from the camp, away from everything that represented any sort of illness or work. Just for one day, he wanted to forget his own limitations, his own potential life limits, and just be a man out on a date with a woman.

"What did you have in mind?" she asked and gave him a crooked smile.

"I didn't really have much in mind other than to spend the day together." Yes, he was Mr. Spontaneity.

"Sounds good to me. By the way, what's the word on Skinny?"

"Bear took him home, but he stayed out of camp because of the bug. Three days in the hospital was about to do him in. Not a man that takes life lying down."

"I'm just glad he did so well," she said. Settling against the back of the swing, she allowed the motion of it soothe her, though right now she didn't seem to need much in the way of soothing. Problems and stress were remarkably absent. All seemed to be right in the world. For now. "Thank you for the treatment. I thoroughly enjoyed it."

"Any excuse to touch a beautiful woman works for me," he said.

"You're a beast, you know that?" she said, but grinned. He was taking all the starch right out of her, and she hadn't even been aware of it. Giving a small kick against the floor, she set the swing into higher motion and tucked her feet beneath her.

"I do," he said and laughed, then pulled her closer. "It's a status I thoroughly enjoy."

The campers left on their day-long trip, and the grounds of the camp were thoroughly, eerily, silent. Mark approached Ellie with a medium-size box in his hands. "Come on, time's a-wasting."

"What are we doing?" she asked.

"It's a surprise, but you'll need your bug spray, a hat and a bottle of water. Swimsuit's optional."

"Optional, eh?" She narrowed her eyes at him, but his playful attitude drew out the lighter side of her. This was going to be fun, whatever it was. "I'll be right back." She returned in minutes with a beach bag slung over one shoulder and sunglasses perched on her nose.

"Let's go." He put on his backpack, then led the way down to the lake. "I thought we could take one of the canoes and have lunch across the lake."

"Oh, that sounds fun."

After securing their items in the bottom of the canoe, they paddled quietly out onto the stillness of the water.

Ellie sat in front, Mark in the back. They moved around the lake for a while, watching birds and other wildlife at the edge of the water. The fragrance of her custom bug spray drifted back to him and the mosquitoes were remarkably absent.

They eased into a quiet cove away from the busy activity farther down the lake and pulled the canoe out onto the rocky shore. Mark opened a bottle of wine he'd brought along, poured a plastic cup full for each of them and handed Ellie one. She sipped and savored the sharp taste on her tongue. Then, without preamble, Mark leaned toward her and kissed her. It began as a quiet exploration, but soon turned hot and demanding. His arms moved around her, and she didn't resist. She'd somehow lost the will to resist him and her own natural needs that blossomed around him. The day seemed to be a time somehow out of time. They had no responsibilities for the moment, no place to be, nothing urgent required their attention. They needed the break, and they were wildly attracted to each other. Who could argue with long, slow kisses on a day like this?

"Ellie, you drive me crazy," Mark said and ran his tongue from the lobe of her ear down to her neck and nibbled his way across the sensitive skin exposed there. She'd removed her shirt to reveal the pink bikini beneath, and he cupped her breast, thumb stroking the peak of her nipple through the clingy fabric.

"Then I know exactly what we need to do," she said and eased back from him.

"What's that?"

Standing, she removed her sandals and eased her shorts down, then kicked them aside. "Have a cold swim! I'll beat you to the water," she said. Picking her way over the few feet to the water's edge, she stumbled into the frigid lake with a squeal.

The chase was on, and Mark dashed after her. She was a few strokes ahead of him, but he swiftly caught her. His daily swims in the lake had begun to pay off.

Catching up to her as she struggled to swim while giggling was easy. In seconds he grabbed her ankle and held on. It was like holding onto a slippery mermaid. Reeling her in, he caught her under the knees, then hauled her closer and clasped her hips to his.

The second their bodies touched, all play ended. Looking down into her dark brown eyes that changed from playful and startled to heavy with desire, Mark knew he was lost to her. He loved this woman with every breath he had in him. Life just wasn't fair. He'd found the woman he would have chosen for himself had he met her under any other circumstances. She was strong and proud, but compassionate and kind as well. She didn't deserve to have a death sentence hanging over her head the way he did. Dammit. The joy of the day fogged over as surely as the afternoon clouds ranging in from overhead.

He pulled away from her and released her legs. She floated away onto her back, uncertainty on her face. Though he wanted her, had wanted to make love to her again, he didn't dare. One chance at intimacy was all they had, and he'd do well to leave her alone now. She didn't deserve the heartache he could bring to her, especially after her previous fiancé had hurt her.

"I'm sorry, Ellie." Releasing her, he swam away, leaving her staring after him as she treaded water.

"Mark? What's wrong?"

The sound of her voice echoed off of the rocks and through his heart. He owed her an explanation, but couldn't form the words in his mind, let alone speak them aloud. This wasn't what he wanted, but he had no choice. He'd never put her or any woman through his illness again. Until his five years were up, he had no choice, and he'd never ask her to put her life on hold for that long. She deserved any chance at happiness that came her way, whether he was in it or not. She'd suffered in the romance department already.

"I think I'm ready to go," he said and hauled himself out of the water onto a rock to dry. The picnic box remained untouched. What a waste. "Maybe this wasn't such a good idea after all."

"What?" She swam over and climbed onto the rock beside him. "What's wrong? One second we're having a good time, then the next second you're acting as if I've developed leprosy. What's up?" She pushed her wet hair up and away from her face.

What could he do, lie to her? She'd felt his touch; she knew the depth of the passion between them when they'd made love. Ellie was not someone he could easily turn his back on, even though he knew he had to. She was smart and vibrant and that's what had attracted him to her in the first place. He wanted to kick himself for allowing himself to touch her, even once. But he would cherish that memory forever.

"I'm simply ready to go back to camp. The water's colder than I thought." The chill in him wasn't due to the temperature of the lake water, but the cold that had lived inside of him for too long.

"Well, we're out of the water and up on a nice warm rock sitting in the sunshine." She crossed her arms and stared at him. "I'm not leaving until you spill whatever it is that's bugging you."

"Me, spill?" he asked. "I have nothing to spill."

"Mark. Just because we've been intimate once doesn't give me the right to tell you what to do, but maybe you could share a little more of yourself with me. It might do you good to talk about it."

"It?" Was he so damned shallow?

"Yeah. Whatever it is that's bothering you." Reaching out, she put the lunch box onto her lap and opened it. "Oh, this looks good. My mouth's watering already."

Unable to resist the aroma, his mouth began to water and his stomach actually growled. His appetite knew no shame. He glanced at her from the side. She was smarter than he thought. Sneaky, too. "You knew I would respond to that food, didn't you?"

"Pavlov ring a bell?" She grinned and held out a cold chicken leg to him and waved it back and forth. "If you want it, you have to answer one question."

"Does that go for you, too? Fair's fair."

For a second she looked as if she would reconsider participating in this game. "I guess. But I go first."

As long as he got that piece of chicken, he'd answer just about anything. He was too easy. "Go ahead."

"What changed your mind back there?" she asked and held the chicken out in front of him.

Sighing, he didn't know if this was a good idea. Then his stomach growled again, and he knew he had to answer her or he was going to starve to death right here and now. "You did."

At her gasp, he grabbed the leg from her, then tore off a bite. Oh, this was good. Bear was a magician, not a cook.

"Me? What did I do?" Stunned surprise remained on her face and her hand lingered in the air with no chicken in it.

"You didn't do anything."

"Then how can you blame your change in behavior on me?" Reaching into the box, she retrieved another chicken leg, but held it without taking a bite. "You're a very confusing man."

He chewed a minute as he thought about how to answer that. "It's because I care about you, Ellie. That's why I stopped." He finished the chicken before she spoke again, and it turned to a cold lump in his gut instead of the nourishment he'd anticipated.

"I don't understand." Tears formed in her eyes and his insides cramped at the sight. "I truly hadn't expected to find a friend here, let alone someone to…care for, but I have. Are you telling me you don't want to take our relationship any further than it already has gone?"

"I'm telling you, Ellie, that I *can't*." His voice had grown gruff with emotion, and he heard it himself, so he knew that she heard it, too. Damn. He hadn't expected this out of today. Selfishly, he'd just wanted to spend some time with her, and now he saw what a big, fat, bad idea that had been. "I didn't mean to mislead you—"

"Then why the hell did you even ask me out if you didn't want to get to know me? What was the point in this? Just something to do so you wouldn't be bored?"

"No. It was nothing like that." Running a hand over his head, he closed his eyes. "It was an impulse, nothing more."

"An impulse?"

Anger snapped in her eyes, and he knew he deserved all of it.

"I'm not buying that. There were days between when you asked me out and now. Why not just cancel the date?" She leaned forward and narrowed her eyes at him. "I know there's something else going on, Mark. Now, tell me."

"We're simply not right for each other." That sounded so lame. "I'm sorry, Ellie."

"Yeah, right. Let me remind you, Doctor, of your own medicine. Just a few days ago you lectured me about opening up and sharing of myself emotionally. Do you recall that conversation?"

"Yes." And he recalled touching every inch of her body while he was at it.

"Then take some of your own medicine. You expect me to open up and unload my problems on you, but you aren't willing to open up and share a little bit of yourself with me? How fair is that?"

"It isn't, and I know it, and I'm sorry." So very sorry that he couldn't put words to how badly he felt. So very sorry that he would never again know her touch.

"And what about all the crap you fed me about taking advantage of everything life had to offer? Was that just for everyone else, not you?"

"No, of course not—"

"Then, what?" Her breathing came fast, and she twisted the napkin in her hand.

Unable to speak what was really in his heart, he remained silent. It was for her sake, not just his, that he couldn't reach out to her any longer.

"Well, okay, then. I guess we're done here." She stood. "Mark, you're a hypocrite. Let's go back to camp." She closed the picnic box and didn't look at him again as they gathered their gear.

He knew he'd hurt her, but he didn't have the words to make it right. He didn't have the time he needed in order to make it right.

The canoe trip back to camp was long and silent and painful for both of them.

CHAPTER FOURTEEN

ELLIE stayed in the lodge after they returned from the lake and sipped a cup of coffee in silence. Rain had begun to drizzle by the time they reached the camp's shore, so she grabbed her stuff and ran. The rain was a good enough excuse to get out of there. She simply couldn't return to the infirmary right now. Not with Mark so close at hand, but so far away emotionally. She hadn't pegged him for an emotionally distant man, not with the way he related to the kids and shared of himself with them. The way he'd risked himself to save Skinny had taken so much more courage than she could ever think of having. She'd been silly to even consider that there had been a chance for them together. The relationship fairy was cruel indeed.

Heavy footsteps approached, but she didn't look up, hoping whoever it was would simply keep moving. A coffee carafe appeared in front of her, and her vision expanded to include Bear. Without a word he placed an empty cup on the wooden table, filled it, then refilled her own.

"Looked like you could use some more." He sat down across table from her and picked up his mug.

She looked down at the steaming black liquid. "I think it's going to take more than a cup of coffee to help me out, Bear."

"I got a bottle of good Irish whiskey in the back for emergencies if you need it. Purely medicinal, you know."

Warmth at the gesture heated her chest. "Thanks, Bear. I'll let you know."

"Good enough." Companionable silence filled the air between them for a few minutes. Ellie listened to the song of the wind through the trees, and mourning doves cooed outside the lodge as the rain continued to drizzle. Though the sounds should induce peace and well-being, she couldn't find it in her. Not now. Not after Mark's announcement. Not after the way her heart had reacted.

"Might not hurt to talk to him," Bear said. He sipped from his cup and sat across the table from her, a great hulk of a man with compassion pouring out of him. Something else totally unexpected from the man.

"What do you mean?" Could he seriously mean Mark?

"Dr. Mark. You need to talk to him."

"Why should I?" Anger now replaced any warmth in her chest. Men always stuck together, didn't they?

"He needs you. He needs to talk to you."

"Believe me, he doesn't need anyone." He'd made that more than clear today.

Bear nodded. "I can see how you might think that, but you're wrong."

"Bear. I tried to talk to him, just today. We were having a good time, then he shut down on me. You can't have a conversation with someone who won't talk."

"Yep. That's the truth of it. Sometimes you just have to talk without saying any words." He scratched his beard and frowned. "Maybe *communicate* is a better word than *talk*."

"You lost me." Were all men so complicated?

"I'm not one much for giving advice. You and Dr. Mark have been good to me, so I hate to see you both hurting."

"Bear—"

He held up his hand for her to stop. "You might not know about this, being a woman and all, but men have fears. When we think we can't do right by our woman or our children, now that's the worst fear of all."

"I don't know what you mean by 'do right by.'" This was confusing her more than ever. A dull pain was beginning at the base of her skull.

"Men take care of things. We get things done. We're not much on feelings unless they're so powerful we can't help it. But give us a job to do, and we can get it done. That's how we show our true feelings."

"I got that. My dad was a fixer. Any problem you took to him, he could fix it or figure out how to get it straightened out."

"See? Your dad was a real man and a real dad."

"He was." Now, thinking of him wasn't as painful as it had been at the beginning of the summer. Time did have a way of healing things, though it was the world's biggest cliché to think of it that way. It was true. The ache that had lived in her heart for him no longer had the influence it once had. At least that was something.

"Now what did he do if he had a problem he couldn't solve?" Bear asked and took another sip.

"Oh, that was bad." She chuckled at a memory. "He wouldn't give up until he figured it out. Not a good time to be around him, either."

"Did he ever have a problem he couldn't fix or solve on his own?"

"Sure. When he was sick. He went to the doctor, but the doctor couldn't fix him, either." Enlightenment struck Ellie, and she stared at Bear. Reaching out, she clasped his wrist and squeezed. "He's trying to protect me, isn't he?" she whispered.

Bear simply smiled, and his eyes curled up at the outer edges. "Might be. A real man takes care of what's his. Sometimes the way we go about things might not be the most intelligent way, but we protect what's ours."

"I'm such an idiot," she said and closed her eyes. She should have seen it. Her father had done the same thing. When he became ill and knew that he wasn't going to be getting better, he went through every insurance policy, every bank account, and ensured that her mother would have everything paid for, everything in order, and there would be no reason for her to worry financially the rest of her life. It was the last thing he could do for her, aside from love her until he no longer could. It was what had made him such a good father and husband. And one of the reasons they missed him terribly. He'd taken care of things until the very last.

"When my mother figured out what he was doing she

was furious. Then she cried, then he cried." She shrugged. "It wasn't what she wanted."

"But it was something he needed to do, right?"

"Yes."

"And somehow they met in the middle, didn't they?" Bear asked.

"Yeah. They were like that. They had their own way of working things out together." She shook her head. "I know I'll never have that."

"Of course you won't."

A pang of disappointment and longing shot through her. "Bear, this would be a good time to reassure me and tell me that I'll find it, right?" That faint hope that had blossomed in her chest faded to dust at his words. She was going to choke that fairy.

"Nope. This would be a good time to tell you to quit moping around in the lodge. I gotta wax the floors before the kids get back. If you want to work things out with Mark, you go after him and do it. If you do, you'll have your own version of what your parents had, just not exactly what they had."

"I see. Thanks, Bear. That was one of the more interesting pep talks I've ever had," she said. Standing, she moved around the other side of the table before he could get up. She leaned over and hugged him, then kissed his cheek. "It was just what I needed to hear."

"Good. Now get outta here. I saw Mark getting ready for a run, so you'd better hurry."

"Thanks!" With a wave she dashed out of the lodge and sprinted for the infirmary. She nearly ripped the hinges off of the squeaky screen door and leaped through the entrance. "Mark! Where are you?"

Only silence greeted her, and she stopped. Damn. She'd missed him, and she had no idea where he'd gone running. "Fooey." Shoulders drooping, she caught her breath. What in the world had she been thinking? No matter what Bear said, Mark didn't want her. He'd made that abundantly clear out on the lake. He had a life elsewhere. Just because they'd made love one time didn't mean that he was going to want to have a relationship with her. How could they have a relationship when they lived so far apart anyway? Long-distance relationships sucked. And hadn't she told herself that she was simply going to take care of herself over the summer and not even think about relationships until the fall?

Well, she hadn't thought, she'd just jumped right in to one. She huffed out a sigh and turned.

Mark stood right behind her, and she shrieked. Grabbing her arms, he hauled her against him. "I don't care if it's wrong. I don't care if I get hurt, Ellie. I don't want you to get hurt. I don't want to hurt you." The fierce look in his eyes would have frightened her once, but now she knew it was fear and not anger behind them.

"Let go of me," she whispered and shook her hands to free them of his grip.

"I shouldn't handle you that way, sorry." He released her.

Reaching out, she grabbed him around the shoulders and pulled him close to her. Automatically, his hands reached for her hips. "No, you shouldn't. I want to put my hands on you and I can't when you're holding them."

On fire, she hooked her hands around the back of his head and dragged his mouth down to hers. She didn't kiss him so much as she devoured him. Parting her mouth she slid her tongue inside his, teasing and tasting him, daring him not to respond to her. With a groan, he pressed her back against the wall and leaned into her. Hands ranged over each other, teasing skin and tugging at clothing.

"Oh, God, Ellie. I want you." His breath was harsh in his throat. Unable to prevent himself, he clasped the straps of her swimsuit and drew them down over her shoulders. When she figured out where he was headed, she gasped and kept her eyes on his. She didn't stop him and didn't look away. The desire in her eyes was a beautiful thing to see.

He'd stopped earlier, but now he didn't know if he could. He certainly didn't want to.

She reached for his hand and pulled it up to her breast. She closed her eyes as he held the soft flesh, brushed his thumb over the hardened peak. She was luscious in her desire and watching her enjoy the passion between them sealed his fate. He loved her.

Somehow his mouth found her breast, and he breathed deep. Aching for her, he pressed his hips against hers, and she rubbed hard against him. She touched his ear with her mouth, and her breath was hot and harsh. "Take me to bed, Mark. Take me to bed, now."

Unable to resist her plea, he moved with her down

the hall to his room and opened the door. Without letting
go of her, he found the bed, and they collapsed onto it.
Clothing and swimsuits flew across the room until there
was only skin between them.

Two o'clock in the morning had always been his be-
witching hour. For whatever reason, when 2:00 a.m.
came, he woke. If he had pain, or dreams, or something
on his mind, no matter if he slept deeply at first, when
2:00 or thereabouts arrived, he opened his eyes.

The same thing happened tonight. He and Ellie had
made love again and it was as magnificent as the first
time. His body had remembered what to do and had less
of a problem figuring things out than his mind did. It
had always been his mind that caused him trouble.

Rising from the bunk, he moved to the kitchen for
something to eat. Though he and Ellie had been together
earlier in the evening, the ability for two people to successfully *sleep* together in one of the bunks was impos-
sible, so she'd moved back to her bed after a long,
lingering kiss by the doorway.

He opened a bottle of soda and sat at the bistro table,
put his elbows on it and dropped his face onto his hands.
How was he going to survive the remainder of the summer without hurting Ellie any more than he already
had? What was going on between them was magical and
totally wrong. There were years left until he could reach
out to a woman and not let go. He had to let go of Ellie.
For her sake, he had to.

A sound drifted into his consciousness, and he

looked up, expecting to see a camper in the doorway. Ellie hovered there instead.

"Are you okay?" she asked.

"Yeah." He turned to face her and smiled. She was all sleepy eyes and rumpled nightshirt, bare legs and feet. What he wouldn't give to be able to crawl into bed with her and sleep away the rest of the night. "I'm okay. Did I wake you?"

"Mm-hmm. It's okay though." Taking a step forward, she placed her hand on his bare back, then sat in the seat beside him. "Sleep's overrated, right?"

"Not in my book."

"Do you want to talk?"

She was giving him an opportunity that he could no longer avoid. He had to talk, had to tell her everything, or he couldn't live with himself any longer.

"I want my life back, Ellie," Mark said and turned away from her. He shoved both hands into his hair and clutched the sides of his head. Agitated didn't begin to describe what he was feeling. "I can't take it anymore. I can't take it."

"Why can't you have a life? I don't understand." She'd gone perfectly still, intently focused on him.

"Because I…I have cancer."

"No, you don't. You told me you were treated and free of disease. You have been for three years." The agitation in her voice made it raise an octave.

"I was. I am." He groaned loud, hating to hear the words come out of his mouth, but they had to be said. "But my life is on terminal hold for another two years."

"Why? What's two years got to do with anything?"

"Until I'm free of cancer for five years I can't have a life or a relationship with anyone, no matter how much I want it. Not even you." There. He'd said it out loud and to the one person in the world he never wanted to hurt. If he wanted to spare her in the long run, he had to do it now.

"Mark, that's ridiculous." She leaned back in the chair, a stunned look on her face.

"Ridiculous? Is that what your mother thought when your father died?"

"Of course not. She didn't want him to suffer any more than he already had. She was grateful, as was I, for the time we had with him."

"Didn't it break your heart to love him and lose him?"

"Yes, it did. But we didn't love him any less because he was only going to be with us a short time. We probably loved him more."

"You were an adult when you lost your father. What would happen if I fathered a child and then died? How fair would it be to that child and the mother? Not at all." He just couldn't do it.

He had to break out of this cage that trapped him, and he left the kitchen and strode to the main room. No matter what Ellie said, no matter how she tried to rationalize things, it wouldn't work. Couldn't work. He wouldn't do that to her or a child. Not the way it had been done to him.

"Mark!" She reached out and stopped his movements. "Stop it. Will you listen to yourself? You have a right to have a life. You have a right to live it." She took a deep breath. "You have the right to love, and be loved, well for as long as possible. We all do."

Trembling from the bound-up rage inside him, he clenched his teeth against the emotional pain that was tearing a hole in him. "I can't, Ellie. I can't. I won't knowingly do that to someone I love." And he knew he loved her or the pain wouldn't be this bad.

"But you have friends, you have family, that love you. You're worthy of being loved, Mark. I don't know where you've been living, but there are no guarantees in this life anyway. I could go back to Dallas and get hit by a bus. Should I have waited until I was certain it was safe to live my life?" Anger snapped in her eyes. "Weren't you the one who lectured me about reaching out to grab life with both hands? And here you are afraid to do it yourself."

He clasped her shoulders. "Ellie, I can't take the chance I'll develop cancer again within the first five years. It's my worst fear, and I simply can't do that to another person. To you."

"What if someone cares for you already and wants you to love them back, no matter what, no matter how much time you have?"

The tears she'd been struggling to hold back brimmed in her eyes. Mark knew what she was saying, knew that part of him wanted to reach out to her, to take what she offered and to hell with the rest of it. Cancer was the bus that was going to run him down.

"I would tell this person that I can't be what they need right now and to find someone who can be."

She jerked away from him and hugged her arms around her middle. "You're being so unfair to yourself. You must know the cure rate by now? Why not simply monitor your blood levels every six months or so? Keep track of it, stay on top of it. Can't it be that simple?"

"I do that already. I just don't know if it will be enough." The fight seemed to run out of him. "I know what it was like to grow up without a father, so I won't willingly or knowingly inflict that loss on a child. He could have made a difference in the lives of me and my sisters, but he chose not to. I won't create a life that I won't be around to raise."

"Do you hear yourself? You sound like the ultimate martyr, sacrificing yourself so that those around you won't have to suffer if you get sick again."

"Say it, Ellie. It's not just sick—it's *dying* from a recurrence of cancer."

"So you think you're the only one who's faced this issue? How many cancer survivors are down on their knees every day, grateful to have just one more day with their families and loved ones?"

Furious, she stormed from the infirmary and ran outside into a rain that neither of them had noticed. Her tears mixed with the rain and dribbled down her face. He was so much more valuable than he knew. Not just in what he could offer someone in support, but in his humor, in his friendship.

"Ellie, I'm sorry," he said.

Surprised he'd followed her, she turned. They were both soaked in minutes. "Don't be sorry, Mark. Go back to your calendar and start ticking off the next two years, and then you can come out of your cocoon."

"Do you think I like this? That I'm enjoying putting any sort of life I might want, any future I want, on hold for two more years?" He grabbed her roughly by the shoulders. "Do you think I want cancer more than I want you?"

"Apparently, you do. You get something out of this or you'd already have taken your life back. You wouldn't let the cancer win. You're a coward, Mark Collins. Somehow, along the way to recovery, you left your courage behind." If he couldn't see it, then there was nothing for them.

"I died, Ellie! Everything in me died when I found out that I had cancer. Then it took whatever I had left to find the strength to survive the treatments. I lost my fiancé. I had to quit my job because I could no longer function."

"I know, Mark. I know. And now, faced with an opportunity to rebuild your life, to make it better than it was before, you don't reach out, you won't take the chance—you simply turn away. When there's someone who loves you standing right in front of you, you walk away because it's easier."

"Easier! Do you honestly want to love someone, start a family even, with someone who might leave you?"

"Who said anything about starting a family, or marriage for that matter? Is that all you want? Right now, all I want is a chance to be with you to see where we might get to, and you won't even take it. There are no guarantees in life, Mark. I could marry someone and have children with him, and he could die in a car accident, or leave me for someone better than me." That had happened to so many of her friends that she didn't even want to think about it.

"There's no one better than you," he said, his voice husky with emotion.

"Then prove it. Take a chance with me, Mark. We have something to build on that I've never experienced in a relationship before. I wasn't expecting to find someone I could love here, and I certainly didn't expect it to happen so quickly. I care deeply for you." Her voice cracked. "But I can't have a relationship on my own. You have to be willing to take a chance on us, take a leap of faith with your future, and reach out for it, no matter the consequences."

Stunned into silence, Mark simply stared at her. The rain appeared unaffected by their storm of emotion and continued to pour down on top of them. "I don't know what to say."

"You've already said it. You've won the battle to save your body, but you've lost the war and let it eat your heart and your soul. If you can't take your life back, no one can do it for you." Calmer now, she wrapped her arms around herself. He'd made his decision, and she'd have to accept it. "I'll write up a schedule for us to divide the clinics. That way we can avoid each other for the rest of the summer."

"I don't want to do that, Ellie."

"Then you'd better figure out what you do want. We've got another few weeks of camp to get through yet, and I won't be able to do my job if we keep on this way."

"I know. Me, either. I didn't expect to find a situation like this."

"What do you mean, 'a situation like this'?" She narrowed her eyes at him.

"Finding someone I could have loved had the circumstances been different."

"Had your attitude been different, the circumstances wouldn't matter." With that, she walked back into the infirmary, and Mark let her go.

CHAPTER FIFTEEN

DAYS passed with Ellie and Mark in a stalemate. They worked together and slept in the same building, but that was about the extent of their interactions.

Carnival weekend arrived and so did Sam and Vicki for their second scheduled trip to camp. This event was planned for the next to the last weekend before camp ended, that way the kids could have a few days to recover from all the fun before heading home.

"Well, I've never seen two more miserable-looking people in my life," Sam said. He and Mark had taken a canoe out onto the lake and left the women to the infirmary with Myra.

"Ellie and I had a bit of a philosophical disagreement." That was a polite way to put it, wasn't it?

"A bit?" Sam barked out a laugh that echoed off the water.

"Okay, a major philosophical disagreement."

"Anything you want to discuss?"

"Not really."

The only sound was of their oars dipping into the

water and the birds chattering in the trees at the edge of the water. A red-eyed common loon lazed about in the middle of the lake, but flipped under the water and swam away at their approach.

"Vicki and I had some trouble over the years, but we worked it out."

"I know, everyone has trouble now and then. But you didn't start out that way. Beginning a relationship with problems only leads to a quick end and pain for everyone."

"But you're crazy about Ellie, I can tell. Being wild about Vicki made me want to work that much harder to keep her with me and happy." He paddled and paused. "To be able to change."

"Yeah. You two were suited to each other from the get-go." Not everyone had the stability that Sam and Vicki had.

"That's possible for you to have, Mark. You've got a lot to offer a woman like Ellie."

"Sure, illness, caretaking when I'm infirm again, holding the bucket for me when I have to take chemo again." Not going there.

"You keep saying *again* like it's a sure thing the cancer's going to come back. Statistics are with you, man. That hasn't hit you yet?" He paused, then returned to paddling. "You haven't had any signs have you?"

"No."

"Then what's your worry?"

"It's like walking around with a guillotine around my neck, just waiting for it to drop. I can't relax or make plans until I know for sure that my life is my own again."

"It's already your own, you're just too afraid to see it."

"Dammit, it's not mine to share. Ellie deserves some-one who can give her what she wants, what she needs, someone to love her the way she should be loved. Not someone with one foot in the grave."

"No one would love her the way you do."

Mark let the pause between them hang. "That's why I have to let her go at the end of the summer."

"Sounds like you've already let her go."

"I guess I have. It's better this way." Didn't mean it wasn't tearing him apart on the inside to do it.

"I respectfully disagree with you, Mark. When we were here a month ago, you were both excited and happy. You were on the verge of discovering what was between you. There was magic in the air around you. Vicki and I both felt it."

"I was deluding myself at the time." Severely.

"About what? Being happy?"

"Yeah. That's what Ellie said, too." The heaviness in his chest grew more dense. This wasn't the way things were supposed to have worked out in his life, but this was what he had gotten. He was just lucky to be alive, and although he immensely appreciated that fact, he wasn't free.

"Think we might be right?"

"No. It's not that I don't have the right. It's just that what happens if we work it out, if we make a good thing between us, then I get cancer again?" He sighed. "I couldn't live with myself if that happened and I died, leaving her to fend without me. If I start something, I intend to finish it."

"Statistics are with you, my friend. I thought you did some research on this."

"I did. I did." Over and over and over.

"You don't believe the research?"

"It's not that I don't believe it—I'm afraid to believe it. What if I'm the odd statistic that doesn't stand up to the research? It does happen and people do die from this, no matter what the statistics read like."

"Then you face life the way the rest of us do, man— no guarantees. You take your chances and grab life with both hands, and you don't let go." Sam half turned in the canoe to face Mark.

"Sometimes having a friend who's a psychiatrist is a royal pain in the ass." Mark jerked his oar forward and splashed Sam a good one.

Sam laughed and shook his head like a wet dog. "I'd have to agree with you on that one."

Mark left the conversation at that point and focused on paddling the canoe, one stroke at a time.

"Guess we ought to head back. They'll be ready for the carnival to start soon and something unexpected always happens," Sam said.

Mark followed his lead, and they turned the canoe back to the camp.

Before the carnival got into full swing, Ellie and Vicki set up a first-aid clinic on the porch of the lodge in readiness for the flurry of bumps and bruises and minor injuries they were sure would occur.

The mail arrived while they were waiting for little

customers, and Ellie accepted the giant mail sack from the postman, as well as a small package addressed to her.

"Oh, this is for Bear," Ellie said after opening the box containing an order of her new essential oils. "He wanted some lavender oil for the kitchen to put on burns right away."

"How is his?" Vicki said.

"It's nearly invisible. At first I was really surprised that it worked so well, but I really shouldn't be. Lavender is such a great oil."

"You did a good job with that. He could have had a serious scar."

"Thanks. I was just surprised that Mark went for a complementary therapy. Most docs I know wouldn't have. Too alternative, not scientific enough." She'd heard that argument for years, but it hadn't stopped her from trying the oils on herself and her friends who were open to new ideas.

"Mark's full of surprises." Vicki grabbed a bottle of water from the ice-filled cooler beside them. Though they were in the shade, the humidity made the air feel hotter.

"Yeah, I know." He'd surprised her in so many ways in the past few weeks, she couldn't keep track. The last surprise she could have lived without.

"Let's sit for a while. The relay races are about to start, so that's pretty benign unless someone wipes out at the finish line."

"Okay." Ellie huffed out a sigh and reached for a bottle of water.

"So, how are you and Mark doing?" Vicki asked the open-ended question.

"We aren't." It was as simple as that. Though they had connected for a while, that connection was now broken in a way that couldn't be mended.

"This is just an observation, but you both look pretty unhappy."

"I can't speak for him, but I'll be glad when camp is over, and we can go our separate ways, get back to what I'm familiar with." Away from the heartache. Although coming to Maine had seemed like a good idea at the time, it had obviously been a mistake.

"What happened? Things were okay when we were here last."

How much should she tell Vicki? Not that she wouldn't guess anyway, so she might as well spill it. "We made love."

"What? *What!*" Vicki leaned forward, intent on hearing everything. "Was it that bad?"

Tears pricked Ellie's eyes, and she gave a sad smile. "No, silly. It was wonderful. That's what makes the situation so bad. We had a wonderful few days, maybe a week, as lovers, then Mark decided that he was more into protecting me than being with me."

"Oh, Ellie, I'm so sorry. Did you tell him he's an idiot?" Vicki placed a comforting hand on Ellie's shoulder.

Tearful, Ellie gave a watery laugh. "Basically. But he doesn't want me to get too attached to him, then have something horrid happen, like his cancer return." She took a gasping breath, still unable to see the logic in his thinking. "He can't see the benefit of being together even if something bad happens in the future. He doesn't see that I could help him, that I would support him, that I would love him no matter what."

"Part of his resistance may be because of his former fiancé."

"Another thing we have in common. He told me about her, and I told him about Alan. I think he's over the hurt of that breakup, but not the fear, and that's something only he can conquer."

A camper with a splinter interrupted their conversation and, from then on, their time was filled with little bits of this and that.

When Vicki dispensed the first aid, Ellie gave a kiss to the cheek of the injured camper. When Ellie treated, Vicki gave a kiss, and they applied a red, red lipstick for each one. Soon there were campers all over the place with lipstick imprints on their faces. Some kids began to fake injuries in order to get another dose of loving from the nurses.

"This is turning into a kissing booth," Vicki said and kissed another cheek.

"We should start charging." Ellie laughed and started to give kisses to anyone that came by.

"Charging for what?" Sam asked as he and Mark approached the first-aid station.

"Kisses," Vicki said and gave Sam a smooch on the cheek.

"Sounds good to me," he said and smooched her back.

They were so good together. They were more comfortable and happy than Ellie had seen them in years. Their lifestyle adjustments had paid off for them in happiness, and she was thrilled that their marriage and friendship had survived the rocky times. As Ellie watched, envy twisted in her, and she glanced at Mark, who also watched their friends. The expression on his face mirrored what was going on inside of her. If she could only convince him to take a chance…

Sudden screams rent the air and the hairs on Ellie's arms stood straight up. She rose and looked around for the problem. Mark's energy reflected that his system was on high alert, too.

Together they stepped off the porch, and Mark reached for her hand. Somehow Ellie had an emergency pack in her hand before she became consciously aware of it.

"Help! We need help over here." A counselor raced over to the lodge and waved for them to follow.

"What's wrong?" Mark asked as he and Ellie ran behind him.

"Ricky's choking."

Oh, no, Ellie thought. One of her worst patient scenarios. If they didn't clear the airway in a few minutes, a child could choke to death right in front of them.

They arrived at the scene to find a crowd of campers gathered around a boy of about ten years of age. Immediately, they could see that this situation was serious. The boy had already lost consciousness, his face a ghastly blue.

"What was he eating?" Mark asked as he shot into action and dropped to the ground beside Ricky.

"Hot dogs." The counselor shoved his hands into his hair and paced back and forth. "We were having a contest."

"Bad idea. Ellie, send someone for the oxygen tank."

"I'll go." The counselor raced away.

Mark didn't waste any time. She'd never seen such focused intensity in him. She assisted Mark to turn the boy onto his back and began a series of chest thrusts to try to dislodge the object occluding the trachea.

She looked into the boy's mouth for anything, but nothing had loosened. "Again," she said, trying to control the anxiety surfacing in her. The boy was turning a dreadful shade of bluish gray now.

Mark again thrust on the boy's chest. "Come on, kid. Come on!"

"Turn him," she said and again checked his mouth. "Nothing."

"Dammit," Mark ground out. "We might have to do a tracheotomy right here."

"Can Sam help you?"

"Yeah, but I'm better at the quick-and-dirty stuff." He cursed nonstop under his breath.

Sam arrived with the oxygen tank, the anxious counselor trailing behind him. "Vicki's calling 911 right now."

"We don't have time to wait," Mark said. Sweat poured out of him from his efforts.

"I'll go get the trach kit," Sam said and ran to the infirmary just a few short yards away.

"Come on, Mark. You can do it. Just one more time,"

Ellie said, urgency, anxiety and somehow hope pouring out of her. "You can do it. I *know* you can."

The glance between them took a split second, but in that time, Ellie gave every confidence, every desire, every spark of powerful energy, she had to Mark. He clenched his jaws together and performed another series of five chest thrusts.

Hands shaking, knowing this was the deciding moment, Ellie looked in the boy's mouth. "Turn him more, there's something there, but I can't get it," she cried. Mark turned the boy to his side, and Ellie scraped out the remnants of a half-chewed piece of food with her fingers. "Oh, you did it, Mark!"

They eased him back and place the oxygen mask over Ricky's face. Ellie's joy turned to fear. "He's not breathing."

"Bag him."

Quickly she switched oxygen devices and pushed oxygen into the boy's lungs with the ambu bag. "You can do it, Ricky, you can do it," she whispered with each squeeze of the oxygen bag. "Come on, buddy, breathe."

Sam returned with the kit that was now unnecessary. "Wow. Good work. You got it."

"Yeah, but he's not breathing on his own," Mark said and reached for Ricky's arm. "Pulse is really fast, but at least he has one." Sweat dripped off of Mark onto the ground.

"Where's that ambulance?" Ellie asked, not looking up from her task, and she took up Mark's cursing under her breath.

"Easy, Ellie. You're doing great. His color's improving, too," Mark said and applied the oxygen monitor to Ricky's finger. "Slow down, take your time and give him good breaths."

"My hands are getting tired." Her arms were shaking from the effort.

"I'll take it for a while." Crawling close to her, Mark placed his hands over hers, and she took his place to monitor the vital signs. The tension between them had evaporated and now they were the team they had been not so long ago. Ellie looked up and met his gaze. They looked at each other for a moment, and she could see the longing in him. A blink of his eyes, and the connection between them broke.

Sirens cut the air and Ellie breathed a sigh of relief. "Oh, thank heaven, they're here."

"Vicki will show them where to come," Sam said.

After they turned Ricky over to the ambulance crew, who took him to the ER for further evaluation and monitoring, a gloom settled over the camp. Even the skies seemed to sense the discord of what should have been a happy day and a light drizzle chased everyone into the lodge. The carnival was over.

Ellie grabbed the equipment and headed to the infirmary with Mark right behind her.

"You did great back there," he said and wiped his hand over his face.

"So did you." She shivered as her wet clothing began to chill her. "I don't think I've ever been so scared. I thought we were going to lose him."

"Takes a real pro to not lose your cool like you did."

"I was just glad it wasn't more hornets," she said and another shiver crossed her flesh. "Ew."

Mark laughed, and Ellie joined him. They needed the break after sharing such an intense case.

"Me, too," he said and took a step closer to her.

She caught her breath, afraid to move, afraid to hope. Her gaze latched on to his and wouldn't let go. "I hate hornets."

He stepped closer still, all playfulness gone in an instant, his green eyes intense and focused on her. "Me, too." With that, he pulled her into his arms and hugged her. "Ellie."

Tremors vibrated through him and into her as she clasped her arms around his back. This was what she needed—to be touched and loved by Mark. And he needed to be touched and loved by her. There was no one else for her, and she knew in her heart that she was what he wanted, too. Somehow she had to convince him of it.

They stood for long moments simply holding each other and coming down from the high anxiety of the shared case. Mark's soothing strokes on her back soon gave her the strength to pull away from him to tell him what he needed to hear and what she needed to say.

"Mark Collins, I love you." Reaching for his face, she pulled him down and laid a gentle kiss on his mouth.

"Ellie."

She stopped him before he could deny her. She had to speak the words in her heart that were bursting to be free. "Whether you love me or not, you must know that

I love you. Vows that are spoken in sickness and in health I give to you now, between just the two of us." Tears formed in her eyes, and she dragged in a ragged breath as the beating of her heart nearly closed off her throat. "With all my heart, with all my soul, I will be with you whether you're healthy or not. I love you and want time with you. What matters is not the amount of days we have together, but the joy and the love within those days that counts."

"Ellie." His voice was a hoarse whisper, and he swallowed quickly.

Desperation was in every movement he made as he reached out and yanked her back into his embrace. He trembled and so did she. The power of the feelings between them nearly scorched the air in the room. If he didn't speak soon, she was going to die of embarrassment right here in his arms. He pulled back and cupped her face with his hands.

"I've never known anyone like you." Energy and passion and love nearly glowed in his eyes. "You mean more to me than I ever thought possible. I don't know what my future is, but without you in it, it's going to be awfully sad and boring."

Tears that formed in her eyes now overflowed down her cheeks, and hope began to ease the ache in her chest. Mark dropped to his knees in front of her and took her hands.

"Let me give back the vows you've just given to me, because they are the most beautiful words I've ever heard." He took a breath and squeezed her hands. "I, Mark Collins, vow to adore you for as long as we have together. We are a beautiful team that no one, not even me, can tear apart. You are the life that breathes within me and keeps my heart beating. Each step of every day I will take part of you with me." He kissed the knuckles of her left hand. "I love you, Ellie Mackenzie. Will you honor me, and marry me, possibly bear my children some day, and love me until the day I die? Whenever that is?"

She drew him up to stand in front of her. Happiness that she'd never experienced in her life filled every cell of her body. "I *do* love you, and I *will* marry you, and we *will* have children and a long, long life together. I just know it."

He pressed a hard kiss to her mouth, then held her against him.

The squeak of the screen door let them know that they weren't alone any longer. "Man, there's just no privacy around here," Mark said and they turned, holding onto each other.

Sam and Vicki came through the door with a sleeping Myra on Sam's shoulder. "What's going on?" Vicki asked, concern etched in her face as she moved toward Ellie. "Did something happen?"

"Yeah." Ellie nodded and looked up at Mark. "We just got married."

"Wh-what!" Vicki yelled and gaped at them.

"Well, not really, but Mark proposed, and I said yes," she replied and squeezed Mark's waist. She wasn't going to let go of him any time soon.

Vicki clasped her hands to her cheeks and turned to Sam, her eyes wide.

"Wow. You work fast," Sam said with a grin and held a hand out to Mark. "Congratulations." He leaned over and gave Eilie a one-armed hug. "To both of you."

"Okay, okay, okay," Vicki said and waved her hands as if trying to make sense of things. "You two sit down right now, and tell us what happened. Last thing we knew you were coming up here to decompress from the emergency."

"I guess we did that, too." Ellie laughed and it was free and happy. "We'll tell you everything, but first I have to call my mom." She reached into her pocket, pulled out her cell phone with a hand that still trembled and dialed. In two rings her mother picked up. "Mom? It's Ellie. I'm getting married!"

"What!" her mother yelled into the phone, and Ellie jerked it away from her ear.

"Why does everyone shriek when I tell them?" she asked Mark.

"Because you are a wonderful person who deserves happiness more than anyone I know," her mother tearfully replied into the phone.

"I'll call you again, later." Ellie finished the conversation in a minute, then hung up.

"We need to celebrate," Vicki said and headed to the kitchen. "Hey! This bag of stuff I brought you weeks ago is still sitting on the counter." She turned narrowed eyes on Ellie.

"What? What bag?"

Vicki pointed to a grocery bag that lay rumpled on the counter, forgotten since it had been left there. "This.

It's part of the stuff I brought you when we were here last time and the stomach flu was running rampant."

"Oh, yeah. I kinda forgot about that bag since everything I needed was in the other one." Confused now, she headed into the kitchen. What could she have overlooked?

"Not *everything*. You're going to have to open it now." Vicki brought the bag out just as Sam returned from putting Myra on a bunk in the ward room. "Sam, they didn't even open my present."

"How rude," he said and grinned. "What present?"

"Present? I didn't know it was a present or I definitely would have opened it. I thought it was just more stomach medicine." She took the bag from her friend.

"Open it." Vicki crossed her arms and tapped a toe, waiting.

Reaching into the bag, Ellie pulled out a bottle of wine and handed it to Mark. "Oh, lovely. We can share it and toast our engagement." She smiled at Mark.

"The rest we're not sharing together. I don't care how much we love you," Vicki said and snickered.

Reaching again into the bag, Ellie pulled out a small box, then shoved it back into the bag with a giggle. "Vicki!"

"Hey, those were meant for you and Mark. If you'd opened the bag at the right time you wouldn't be turning three shades of red now."

"Just why *is* she turning three shades of red?" Mark asked and reached for the bag that Ellie shoved behind her back.

"No reason."

Before Ellie could think, Mark grabbed her around the waist and took the bag from her, opened it and laughed.

"Am I the last one to know?" Sam asked.

Mark hugged Ellie to him while he continued to chuckle and handed the bag to Sam.

"Hey! We could use some of these, too." He looked at Vicki. "Just because we're married, and they're not, doesn't mean they get all the fun."

She reached up and gave him a quick kiss. "True. Very true."

Mark looked at Ellie, and the future no longer held fear for him. With Ellie by his side, he knew that he could conquer whatever challenges life and his health threw at him. "How do you feel about moving to New Mexico? Or I could move to Dallas?"

"My home is where you are. New Mexico has fond memories for me."

"With you there, I think we'll make some more."

"Absolutely."

He kissed her, seeming to find doing so in front of his friends, who witnessed the love between them, a vow, sealing his love for the woman who would soon be his bride.

"You know, Sam and I renewed our vows here at camp. Gil even gave us the use of the main house and grounds for a week before they closed things up for the winter. He might be willing to extend the same offer to you."

"My mom and brothers will kill me if I get married without them." Although enticing, the idea might not work for everyone.

"Then invite everyone here for the ceremony. Have a collective family reunion or something," Sam said. "I think we can swing a long weekend, then. How about over Labor Day? Most people are off an extra day for that anyway."

"What do you think?" Ellie asked Mark. The light in her eyes nearly brought him to his knees. He would do anything for this woman who loved him.

"I'm up for it. All we can do is ask Gil and ask the family to come." He brought her hand to his mouth and kissed her knuckles. "I want to marry you, Ellie. I don't care where or when, but I will be there."

Vicki whispered in Sam's ear, then he nodded. She looked at them and cleared her throat. "You know, Sam and I have reservations at a lovely bed-and-breakfast in town. Since Myra's already asleep, why don't you two take our reservation for the night? We can handle anything that comes into the infirmary for one night."

"Vicki, Sam? Are you sure?" Ellie asked. The generosity of their friends was overwhelming.

Reaching out, Mark grabbed the key that Vicki dangled in front of her. "They're sure, now go pack a bag." He nudged Ellie toward her room. "All you're going to need is your toothbrush and that bag of stuff Vicki bought you."

"Mark!" She giggled as she walked down the hall. "I think I need a little more than that."

"Okay. A bottle of aromatherapy oil, but no more than that," he said and turned toward their friends. "Thank you. We'll owe you one."

"Just be happy. That's all the thanks we need." Vicki embraced him and then Sam did as well, with a hearty clap on the back.

"We'll do that," Mark said and knew that it was going to be true.

EPILOGUE

Just a few weeks later

SAM stood with Mark, who fidgeted, on the dock by the lake. "Are you okay, man?" he asked.

"Yeah," was Mark's tight-lipped response. "I'm good."

"You'd better hold onto me, because when you see her, you're going to want to faint. I don't want you to fall in and drown on your wedding day."

Mark laughed and some of the tension in him lifted, the positive energy of the day now filling him again. "I won't, I promise."

Vicki and Myra walked down the path to the lake dressed in matching summer dresses. "Now I think *I'm* going to faint. They're so beautiful," Sam said.

"Be strong."

"You're next," Sam said and gave a small wave to his daughter, who waved back.

"I sure hope so." Mark's dreams of a family of his own were uncertain, as was his future, but at least he was beginning by marrying Ellie. She was his family and his future. The rest would fall into place as long as they loved each other.

When Ellie appeared, Mark's heart, which had been doing fine, began to race in his chest. Each pulse he heard in his ears until it drowned out any other sound. He was hers; there was no doubt about it.

Soft and dreamy in a beige summer dress and sandals, she looked like a dark-haired fairy come from the forest to tempt him. Giving in to the temptation, he held out his hand to her and brought her by his side, where she would remain the rest of their lives together.

"Friends and family of Ellie Mackenzie and Mark Collins, you have been invited here to this grove to witness the love shining between these two people who have promised themselves to each other." The words rang out and were forever etched into the hearts of Mark and Ellie.

At the end of the reception in the lodge, Skinny turned to Bear. "Think I could work in the infirmary next year?"

Bear frowned at the man. Had he gone daft? "No. You're not a doctor or a nurse. Whatcha want to do that for?"

"There's so much romance going on in there, I was hoping some of it might rub off on me."

Bear laughed and clamped his arm around Skinny's shoulders. "Sorry, son. You're stuck with me and the boys in the lodge. We're as romantic as you're gonna get."